JF

RX

FALKIRK COMMUNITY TRUST

30124 02671899 1

Falkirk **Community Trust**

0 2 OCT 2018

1 2 NOV 2018

3 DEC 2018

1 5 AUG 2019

CANCELLED

0 6 SEP 2022

– 4 SEP 2023

KU-750-397

Bo'ness
01506 778520

Bonnybridge
01324 503295

Denny
01324 504242

Falkirk
01324 503605

Grangemouth
01324 504690

Larbert
01324 503590

Meadowbank
01324 503870

Slamannan
01324 851373

Falkirk Community Trust is a charity registered in Scotland. No: SC042403

This book is due
for return on or
before the last date
indicated on the
label. Renewals
may be obtained
on application.

SPECIAL MESSAGE TO READERS

THE ULVERSCROFT FOUNDATION
(registered UK charity number 264873)
was established in 1972 to provide funds for
research, diagnosis and treatment of eye diseases.
Examples of major projects funded by
the Ulverscroft Foundation are:-

- The Children's Eye Unit at Moorfields Eye
  Hospital, London
- The Ulverscroft Children's Eye Unit at Great
  Ormond Street Hospital for Sick Children
- Funding research into eye diseases and
  treatment at the Department of Ophthalmology,
  University of Leicester
- The Ulverscroft Vision Research Group,
  Institute of Child Health
- Twin operating theatres at the Western
  Ophthalmic Hospital, London
- The Chair of Ophthalmology at the Royal
  Australian College of Ophthalmologists

You can help further the work of the Foundation
by making a donation or leaving a legacy.
Every contribution is gratefully received. If you
would like to help support the Foundation or
require further information, please contact:

THE ULVERSCROFT FOUNDATION
The Green, Bradgate Road, Anstey
Leicester LE7 7FU, England
Tel: (0116) 236 4325

website: www.foundation.ulverscroft.com

THE APPLEJACK MEN

Ruben Byrd is wrongly arrested for acts of treachery. To prove his innocence and find the men responsible, he has to break out of military prison. But when he eventually catches up with his target, he realizes that things have changed . . . In the town of Vinegar Wells, the sheriff proposes a two-day bail for the real turncoats to be brought to book, and Ruben has little choice but to accept. With a suspicious quarry in front of him and grasping hunters behind, however, he finds himself in a perilous situation . . .

Books by Caleb Rand
in the Linford Western Library:

THE EVIL STAR
WOLF MEAT
YELLOW DOG
COLD GUNS
THE GOOSE MOON
THE ROSADO GANG
LIZARD WELLS
WILD MEDDOW
BUZZARD POINT
SILVER TRACK
RISING RED
CODY'S FIGHT
CALVERON'S CHASE
STEARN'S BREAK

CALEB RAND

◆

THE
APPLEJACK
MEN

Complete and Unabridged

LINFORD
Leicester

First published in Great Britain in 2015 by
Robert Hale Limited
London

First Linford Edition
published 2018
by arrangement with
Robert Hale
an imprint of The Crowood Press
Wiltshire

Copyright © 2015 by Caleb Rand
All rights reserved

A catalogue record for this book is available
from the British Library.

ISBN 978–1–4448–3632–5

Published by
F. A. Thorpe (Publishing)
Anstey, Leicestershire

Set by Words & Graphics Ltd.
Anstey, Leicestershire
Printed and bound in Great Britain by
T. J. International Ltd., Padstow, Cornwall

This book is printed on acid-free paper

FALKIRK COUNCIL LIBRARIES

1

The cold eased grudgingly from the earth. Fifteen minutes later, the carpet of mist thinned, slowly drifted off south from the clammy ground. In a broad hollow at the rear of the town, a platoon of the Arkansas Volunteer Militia slowly uncovered from its night huddle.

The landscape changed from its shadowy darkness of greys and browns, and the army stirred. Men looked from channels of liquid mud to what were becoming passable lanes and coach roads. Beneath their feet, a nameless creek purled ochre beneath its low cut banks. During the long night some of them had peered across its mournful blackness, saw the red glister of distant campfires and burning timbers.

Jonesboro had been under siege for a month, pulverized by the deadly gunfire of Buckley's Runners. The Confederacy had lost the initiative in the War, and the Louisiana command had asked for the Volunteer Militia to help defend their temporary supply camp.

As the surly, bone weary infantrymen slumped against the cottonwoods in the depression, their tired eyes were on their young officer as he spoke of their next move.

'It's not goin' to be any easier,' the lieutenant growled. He lifted his grimed, unshaven face and stared considerately at his men. Though he was only twenty-four, Timon Timms looked fifty. He'd done battle with Union generals, and fought along the Mississippi with the war dogs of Max Lambert. Each skirmish had ended the same way, with bugles and yells for retreat.

'Sir?' a lightly bearded youth spoke up. 'What's brought Buckley here? Why's he come this far south?'

'I don't know. Perhaps it's you he's after.' Timms replied. 'But he is here, an' he's got a price on our heads. We're not regulars, so them cussed Yankees think we signed up because we're bushwhackers . . . some sort o' guerrillas.'

The men no longer felt like an upfront, gung-ho outfit of confident volunteers, and their tired faces twisted grimly. Three months earlier, they were one of the most proficient fighting units in the Confederate Army, going to end the war before the Yankees knew what hit them. But not anymore. Their battle spirit had worn thin, their potency blown. All they wanted now was an end to the death and destruction, a return glimpse of the peaceable Little Missouri Valley, 120 miles north.

At the edge of the hollow, Ruben Byrd looked out on the rain-sodden ground. He'd heard it all before. The last minute call to make a near suicidal run into a wall of fire with guns exploding, managing their power for the final breach. And he'd witnessed the outcome — more Arkansas blood colouring the soil, augmenting the

3

creeks and rivers — thin lines of bedraggled men being cut down like corn before the sweeping scythes. He dug his hand into a sweat-soaked shirt pocket and withdrew a twist of Brown Mule. He bit deep into the plug and began to chew.

'Byrd,' Timms called, his face carrying more exasperation than anger. 'If you want to walk away from this hole in one piece, listen up.'

Ruben brought his wandering mind back to the lieutenant. He gripped his rifle-musket and spurted a short stream of tobacco juice.

'The captain wants a last assault,' Timms advised. 'The platoons are ready . . . troops are waiting behind. As soon as we do our job they'll advance. If all goes well, Buckley an' company will be no longer.'

'If all goes well . . . according to plan . . . with God's help . . . ' That's all Ruben had been hearing for months. Trouble was, while Union troops were sighting their twelve-pound cannons, everyone who could help out, including Lady Luck, had either turned deaf ears or were looking the other way. Ruben spat another expressive stream of juice.

'This time, we'll be riding in. Let some o' you show your grit,' Timms added.

Ruben brightened slightly, an ironic grin creasing his face. At least it would be fighting the way they knew best. None of the Arkansas men were used to infantry work, and slogging through the Louisiana mire had wearied them as much as facing the enemy. They had all volunteered as a mounted unit and expected to be used as such. But the Southern generals and brigadiers had decreed different, held the army had its own seasoned cavalrymen.

Ruben raised his head to the sky as the early breezes rustled the leaves of the nearby trees. He took off his slouch hat and ran his fingers through his long, fair hair. There was another ominous gather of grey cloud overhead, and he wondered how far off they were from

5

another big rain. His blue eyes squinted as he followed the flight of a jay winging swiftly across the hollow.

'Get the hell out an' don't come back,' he muttered.

The morning mist had cleared now, and the very tops of the cottonwoods were silhouetted as the first rays of the sun broke across land far to the east.

Lieutenant Timms continued outlining the imminent attack. The platoon was to ride on the flank as the main body divided in two to draw the opposition into a trap. Security of the plan was vital to its success. If Buckley was to learn of their deployment, the Volunteers would be cut to pieces. Wishing them luck, the young officer looked quickly to the sky.

'Keep your powder dry,' he advised in acknowledgment of the closing weather. 'Shake out an' saddle up,' he then ordered.

Ruben lifted himself from the ground. He straightened wearily, stretched his lean frame and filled his lungs with the new day's air. His eyes searched the faces of his comrades as they passed. Rubbing a dirty hand over the stubble on his chin, he understood the uneasy silence and fell in with them.

'What you thinkin', Rube?' Jim Robie asked as they sloshed through the mud to the picket rope. 'You reckon we're seein' the end o' this ruckus?'

'Oh, yeah, this one should just about do it, Jimmy. This time next week we'll all be back home, lifting catfish,' Ruben responded facetiously. 'For chris'sake, why should it be any different from the last time or the time before that?' he snapped, this time with sincere feeling. 'I'm sick of this whole goddamn campaign. It seems to me it's a big chess game for the generals . . . wagering on how many of us they can get knocked over. An' is ol' Bluebelly Buckley ever getting bored with killing us? Do you think he'll see the error of the ways, an' invite us to a clambake this Saturday night?'

Robie threw him a sharp glance but clamped his jaw shut. Many of the Volunteers felt the cynicism and the same dark humour, but nobody was going to express it.

'Like the captain ordered, an' no going it alone,' Timms shouted. 'One wrong move an' we'll all be shot to hell.'

'I'll remember you said that,' a raggedy private muttered under his breath. 'If we don't make it, I'll come back as a buzzworm an' strike your goddamn pecker.'

Within a few minutes, the men were ready and mounted, and Timms waved them forward. As a fighting group they looked rag-tag. There was no uniform and most of them wore grey or butternut homespuns. Their black, felt hats were supposed to be adorned with the badge of the Volunteers or a yellow pompom. But after the recent skir-mishes many were without headgear of any description. They travelled light, carrying their scant belongings rolled in a bandolier blanket across their back.

The sound of the horses was muffled as they rode from the hollow to the water-filled ruts leading to the fields beyond Jonesboro. In the distance, a trumpet sounded thinly, its quality more a despondent proposition, than a strident call to action. And then, as the horsemen rounded a long bend in the creek, the peace of the morning was shattered by a sudden barrage of gunfire.

* * *

Screaming bloodthirstily, an advance party of Buckley's Runners broke from the surrounding trees, and fell on the Arkansas Volunteers. All the confident, verbal skills of lieutenants and captains were immediately thrown to the winds, as panicked riders scattered under the onslaught.

Gripping his Colt tightly, Ruben cursed and spun his horse from the trail. Behind him he heard the anguished cries of his comrades as the blue-coated Runners rode in amongst them. As he drew a bead on one, he saw Timon Timms cut from his horse by a swipe from a gleaming Union sabre. Ruben ground his jaw as the big gun bucked in his hand, and the Yankee cavalryman crashed from his saddle. He fought to regain control as his sorrel snorted and wheeled away. Then within moments, as quickly as it began, it was over. He was alone, still cursing, galloping through heavy, trailside timber.

Patchy gunfire rang out as Ruben regained control, turning back through the trails, searching for survivors of his platoon. The wild, warring clamour of a cavalry unit died away as the Raiders swept on towards the main group of Volunteers who were forming up somewhere ahead. His stomach heaved as he came across his comrades. He reined in and looked around him. A mirthless grimace moved his face slightly as he looked down on the rest of his group. Lieutenant Timms, with a gash from the side of his head across to his chest, was sprawled close to Private George Robie. Scattered in the crushed meadowland were more bodies, some face up, some face down. Ruben's wretchedness gave way to anger, and as the blood raced hot through his body he heeled his mount fiercely.

'Goddamn knew it. The end game,' he rasped, heading off to where he thought the main body of Volunteers would be.

The sun had fully broken through the clouds, and its fragile rays glistened on the damp grass. Ruben had made an almost half circle of town buildings, was now at the edge of Jonesboro farmland. He was behind the river, screened by a low bluff, looking across shallow water at a landscape of bloody slaughter. In the hour or so he'd been riding in search, his worst fears had been realized. John Buckley and his Runners had made their surprise assault, charging while the Volunteers sat long-sufferingly waiting to ride forward.

'The end game . . . looks like checkmate, Generals,' Ruben muttered with vicious irony.

The element of surprise that the Arkansas Militias had intended was lost, but a mile to the north, the battle was still raging. Ruben stared numbly at the carnage. On the carpet of smashed-down land, the lifeless heaps of dead and dying looked like collapsed tents across the battlefield. Uncertain of what to do or where to go, he let his mount pick its way through the twisted bodies, watched silently at its decision to forgo uprooted turnips because of the smell of fresh blood.

Ten minutes later, the battle swung around in a wide circle and without any relevant awareness, Ruben found himself in the thick of it. Firing instinctively he rode on, his will to survive doing his thinking for him. The cries of the wounded rose through the stench of death, the cordite fumes that seemed to embrace the damp earth. The shouts of pain and profanity, the startled whinnying of the horses pierced the fog of his brain. A bullet ripped through his shirt, tearing out a chunk of shoulder flesh. But he was insensible to pain, hardly heard the shouting, the cannon fire drumming on his ears. His horse had fallen into a lope. He rammed his empty Colt back into its holster, gripped the reins tighter, swaying with the movement.

'Here we are, fellers . . . told you it wouldn't hurt much,' he said, thinking he'd passed into the other world.

Ruben was beginning to accept the situation when an unfamiliar voice hollered out.

'Over here.'

Ruben shook his head. Clearing some of the mental confusion, he peered in the direction of the shout.

A Confederate officer with a long-barrelled rifle was waving at him. As he snapped back to reality, Ruben now felt the shock, the searing pain of the wound in his shoulder. He looked at the bloodstain and cursed, urged the horse towards the remnants of his company. When he reined in, hands reached up and pulled him roughly from the saddle, dragged him to the stands of oak and cottonwood at the edge of a half-ploughed field.

He propped himself on his good arm, saw hostile, threatening faces looking down at him. He was about to ask what was happening, when the officer forced his way through the soldiers.

'Who the hell are you?' the man demanded.

'Byrd. Third platoon. Who the hell are *you*?' he answered.

The officer glared, appeared to disregard Ruben's impertinence. 'Where'd you come from?'

'Back from their lines, is where,' someone said. The tone was cold, but held plenty of allegation. 'He's one o' them . . . a goddamn bluebelly.'

Ruben blinked. The officer had dropped to one knee, and with his gun hand drawing the bayonet end of his rifle in close, he glowered at Ruben. 'So

14

where's the rest o' your platoon?'

The hardness of the officer's eyes stunned Ruben. 'Gone, sir,' he replied a moment later. 'The yanks hit us before we knew what was happening.'

'How'd they know where you were?'

'I don't know that they did. They had the luck of surprise . . . we didn't.'

'An' how come he's the only survivor?' another voice snorted.

'You got an answer to that, soldier boy?' the officer asked.

'No. I mean, I'm not the one to ask, am I?'

'Oh, I think you are, trooper Byrd. Let me help. Two of our men were seen headed towards the Buckley Runners. I didn't find out about it, nor did the captain until it was too late. I guess some of us are figuring you was one of 'em.'

'How the hell do you figure that? The only man I've rode with recently is back in the trees kissing the ground because most of his chest's missing,' Ruben snarled. 'How I got out I don't know, but I did. You think I'm a conspirator . . . conspiring with the enemy? We was pinned down, three or four miles back, so how the hell could I be?'

'We know the bluebellies had good prices on our heads,' the officer stated. 'Some would say flattering prices. Certainly more'n the forty a month a Private gets.'

With one hand pressed to the wound in his shoulder, Ruben forced himself to his feet.

The soldiers formed an intimidating half-circle around him. Some loosened their Colts, some ran the balls of their thumbs along their rifle bayonets. Without a sound they returned his gaze, open loathing showing in every face.

Beads of sweat trickled down Ruben's forehead. He wiped his hand across his mouth and swallowed hard. He turned his eyes to his bloody wounded shoulder and the pain throbbed worse. Slowly he held out his blood-caked hand.

'Come and take a look. See if you think I shot myself,' he said. 'And if you find more coin on me than makes up a full dollar, you can keep it, you brainless sons-of-bitches.'

The officer considered for a moment, then shook his head.

'All that's as maybe,' he said. With a quick movement of his hand, he waved two of the soldiers forward.

Ruben's hands were held tight behind his back, the jerking stretch of his shoulders tearing excruciatingly at his wound. He gritted his teeth and hissed at the pain, made no effort to fight the hands that held him.

'You'll have your chance, Byrd. If *that is* your name.'

The heavy-set corporal who held his wrists down coughed and spat. 'If I had my way, I'd string him up here an' now. Low-down Yankee liar.'

'If you had your way, we'd all be carrying clubs and grunting,' Ruben snapped angrily.

The officer turned sharply on the

corporal. 'That's enough, Arkie. Right now he's a prisoner ... my prisoner. He can be tried when he gets back to Arkansas.'

Ruben stiffened. 'What in hell's got into all of you? Panic's scrambled your senses. You've got no reason to suspect me of anything. I've told you, I'm from the third platoon. Timon Timms was my Lieutenant. It was me who ... '

'Save your breath,' the officer said. 'We know about you ... who was in the platoon. You're headed for a tribunal, a goddamn court-martial. We'll soon find out who it was you were in cahoots with. Arkie, get him back to the advance post. They'll deal with him. Meantime, I'm going to find Captain Lines. That's if he's still alive. We'll have to reform ... try an' fight our way out of this chaos.'

Ruben wanted to protest. He opened his mouth to say something but knew it was a waste of time. He felt his hands being tied with a rawhide thong, and as he was pulled towards his mount he felt the enmity, saw the antagonism in the soldiers' eyes.

He was hauled roughly into the saddle. Arkie Munce held the reins, and a trooper rode alongside. He gripped his horse's flanks with his thighs, shook his head with incredulity as the three of them headed north. Neither of the guards spoke. Their heads were turned away from him, and a cold shiver ran down his spine. With none of his platoon alive to prove his innocence, and in the custody of a vindictive corporal, Ruben didn't think much for his transient health.

Ten minutes later, Ruben saw the blue jay again. This time it was flying in the opposite direction.

'I bet it was you told 'em about us, you son-of-a-bitch,' he said. 'Even down to the right goddamn colours.'

2

The smell of the old straw in the mattress made Ruben heave. From the high window a finger of yellow light cracked the gloom. For two weeks he had lain in the dirt-floored cell at Fort Clinton.

Easing his stiff body, he let his feet fall to the floor. He leaned forward and tried to stand, but the pain across his ribs made him gasp. Every day he'd been paid a visit by the guards and fort doctor. They came three at a time, always with the same questions as the doctor applied fresh dressings to his wounds. Who'd been his partner? How much were they paid and what had they done with the money? And in response to his protestations of innocence, he got the same treatment. More bruises and more bleeding for the doctor to patch up the following day.

Ruben raised his lean, dirt-grimed face and groaned. His bright, watchful eyes were now dulled and bloodshot. Using his good hand to press himself up, he staggered to his feet. Shuffling across the floor, he went to the corner of the cell and lifted the beaker from the water bucket. He drank, wincing as his injured lips came into contact with the cool tin.

As he threw the beaker back into the pail, he heard the rattle of the lock, the heavy bolt being drawn back. 'Oh, Christ,' he muttered 'Not again.'

'OK, Byrd, get yourself to the door,' a voice called.

'What's up now?' Ruben mumbled. 'You got more work for the doc?'

'Yeah, anytime, but right now the Colonel wants to see you. Hurry up.'

Moving heavy-footed across the cell, Ruben lifted a hand against the glare of the sunlight that streamed through the opening. At the doorway he was stopped and one of the guards held a rifle on him. Another one kneeled, clamped leg-irons around his ankles.

'Just so's you don't get any ideas,' he sneered.

Breathing deep and painful, Ruben tried to hold himself erect. But the bruising on his body was such that he couldn't, not even square his shoulders. He was bent like an old man, stumbling forward under the thrusts and taunts of the two guards.

Under the charges of cowardice and treachery, he'd been held in solitary confinement. Now, he sensed the eyes of the other prisoners boring into him. They were there for the usual variety of reasons, insubordination and fighting, going AWOL. But they were still fighting men, soldiers of the Confederate Army. Had the order been given, they would have fallen on Ruben and ripped out his arms and legs. A lot of them had lost friends and kin at Jonesboro. A Southern traitor was insufferable, and they wanted to see someone swing. Ruben kept his eyes to the front, ignoring the curses and insults that were hurled at him.

As they neared the low, clinker-built offices, the guards paused. Standing in the far corner of the fort quadrangle was a gallows, its noose unmoving and very graphic.

'They fixed that up a few days ago,' one of the guards leered. 'Just for you.'

'Yep. One o' the finest uses a length o' hemp will ever be put to,' his colleague added. He jabbed his rifle into Ruben's ribs, laughing as the prisoner retched with pain.

Ruben turned and looked up. The man's lip was curled over a broken tooth, but the cruel viciousness of his work was stamped all over his face.

'I hope your ugly mug isn't the last thing I see,' Ruben said. 'No one deserves that.'

The man's eyes narrowed as he considered an answer. 'You won't be so pretty when your tongue's swellin' from your double-crossin' mouth,' he growled.

The rifle was jabbed into Ruben

again and he was pushed through a door to the adjutants' block. He was marched down the hallway to the end door; in answer to the guard's knock it was opened and he was taken inside.

Sitting behind a polished table were three officers. Colonel Richmond, the whiskered commander of the Arkansas Volunteer Militia sat in the middle, beside him two captains. Their eyes stared at him with cold indifference.

'Prisoner, attention.' A lieutenant standing at the end of the table barked out the command, and as Ruben brought his heels together, the leg-irons jangled dully on the puncheon floor.

'Sir. Private Ruben Byrd,' the officer reported. 'Third platoon, Arkansas Volunteer Company. Arrested at Jonesboro in the field of battle. Charged with desertion under fire, cowardice and forwarding the enemy information for pecuniary gain. Sir.'

The colonel lowered his eyes to the papers before him to read the account.

Slowly he lifted his head, sniffed and stared at the prisoner. 'Doesn't come much worse than this, does it, Private Byrd? I assume you've got something to say?'

'Well, I'm not accepting it . . . pleading guilty, if that's what you're asking,' Ruben snapped back, his voice suddenly firm. Overcoming the pain, he squared his shoulders and looked the colonel straight in the eyes. 'Someone's making a hell of a mistake.'

Without replying, Colonel Richmond turned to the officer on his left.

'Sir. He was arrested by Lieutenant Schaffer on the morning in question,' the captain advised. 'He was seen coming from the enemy lines. He has protested his innocence, and says he was the only survivor of his platoon. He was wounded in the action and attests an effort to link up with the rest of the company. Sir.'

'All right, Byrd, we'll hear your story,' the colonel said. 'This is a preliminary hearing to see whether you'll be tried by a full court martial. It would be better if you told the whole truth and nothing but.'

Ruben recounted the events of the fateful morning in a monotone. He went through the surprise attack, his own wounding and seeing Lieutenant Timms cut down. At the mention of this, the colonel looked at his papers and nodded.

'We found Timms. It looks like he was killed as you say he was.'

To Ruben, this was at least one bit of compatible evidence. He continued more positively, explaining the time he was beckoned by the officer, Lieutenant Schaffer.

'I don't know what's happened, sir. But someone turning traitor would explain how and where we were jumped. I swear it wasn't me, though. And no court . . . not even a military one . . . can find or prove me guilty because I'm not. That's about it.'

The colonel looked at Ruben, rubbed his jaw thoughtfully.

'Hmm, I don't think so,' he muttered, then indicated that Ruben be stood back against the wall.

The next half-hour took away any slight confidence he'd gained. Six witnesses were called, each one giving his story of the morning's events. All of them testified that one of the traitors had been riding a sorrel and that he looked like Ruben, even describing the clothes he wore. The three officers eyed Ruben. The description fitted the tattered, louse-ridden gear he was still wearing, but no more than it would any number of men from the wiped-out platoon. They were dead though, Ruben wasn't.

He was led outside to stand in the hallway while the summing up was done, the wait for the verdict. After only two minutes, he was taken back inside. Colonel Richmond looked up, his mind made up, his face determined.

'Private Byrd. We have reached our decision,' he stated. 'We feel there is enough evidence for you to be tried by a court martial. Your story is corroborated by small points, but that doesn't mean you couldn't have been with the enemy when the attack on your platoon took place. Though it's not up to me, I think you're guilty.'

Ruben felt his heart thumping, took short, gulping breaths. He didn't think Colonel Richmond and his staff would go through with it . . . put him up for a court martial. His reward for staying alive was to become the fall guy, the officer's scapegoat.

In his dark miasma, he felt himself being dragged down the hall and back out to the quadrangle. As he was marched back to the cell block, a troop of cavalry passed. He was pulled to a halt and the guards yelled out who he was, the outcome of the hearing. Lifting his head, he watched as the horsemen rode past. Some of them spat, others showed little feeling in their fight-hardened faces.

He was shoved into the stinking cell and the door slammed shut. He stared into the gloom, vacantly at the wall ahead of him. To the generals, he was a casualty of the war, he thought. Two men had turned traitor, and through being in the wrong place at the wrong time, he was accused of being one of them. Unless something happened soon, he'd be dancing at the end of an Arkie Munce rope.

* * *

A week of days and nights had passed since Ruben's appearance before Colonel Richmond. To hang on to a positive thought pattern, Ruben had gone fishing. In real time, between beatings, he let his mind hang for brook trout in his homeland streams. It was interminable and good, a contrived distraction from his likely fate. His visits from the guards grew more numerous, sometimes with input from one of the more brutal elements of the Fort's garrison. But he grew used to it, learning to soak up the punches and bootings, rather

29

than fight back. He was actually stronger and harder, but what his jailers saw was a Ruben Byrd who stirred himself as though they had broken his body and spirit.

Unwittingly, they had given him time to formulate a plan. He had noticed there was a weakness in their watch schedule. In the late evenings, an hour after the beating that always accompanied his biscuit and gravy, a lone guard returned. His job was a prisoner check, throw in the threadbare blanket that was Ruben's covering for the night. Now, as he lay on the rank mattress, Ruben's aching muscles tensed. *Come on, you son-of-a-bitch, he thought. It's tonight and you haven't a goddamn clue.*

Well into full dark, he heard the guard outside the darkened cell and he got lightly to his feet. He went to the door, pressing himself against the wall, holding his breath in anticipation. He flexed his fingers, and as the lock was opened and the bolt slid back, he prepared himself to make his move. For the first time in many weeks, he allowed himself a brief smile.

Creaking on its iron hinges, the door opened, and the guard swung his arm in.

'Wrap this around you, Mr Crawfish. You'll soon be usin' it as a shroud,' the voice snarled, indicating a blanket in his hand.

Springing from the wall, Ruben grabbed the arm tight, and in one movement, heaved. The startled guard was pulled into the gloom and before he could shout, Ruben's right fist slammed powerfully into the side of his neck. Ruben grabbed for the man's uniform with both hands, swung him round and up against the cell wall. Then he moved in close, gave short, powerful punches to where he knew there was flesh and bone.

The guard fell to the ground and Ruben took a step back, kicked the same places.

'That's returned interest. I wish I had

it in me to do you more harm,' he growled, wincing with pain. He grabbed the blanket, straightened up and moved quickly to the door to listen. There was a murmur of voices filtering across the darkened quadrangle. But a quick look showed there was no one was close, and without hesitating, he ran to the nearest east side wall of the fort.

Picking his way carefully, he edged along the wall to the rear middle of the fort. The double gates that led to the corral were open, and the guard wasn't at his post.

Safe enough, he thought. *No one's going to break into a fort, are they? And why the hell would anyone be breaking out? Unless they're me.*

He cursed quietly. Using available shadow from the fort's out-buildings, he hurried to the corral, grabbed a saddle from the cap pole and threw it over the nearest horse. The horse whinnied, tentatively shifting its hoofs in the sandy dirt.

'Let's go take a ride, eh, feller,' he

said quietly, his fingers working hurriedly to buckle the belly strap.

Though it felt like hours, he was finished in only a few moments. Then, with a mix of extreme watchfulness and fear, he walked the horse out to the nearest timber stands. Breathing more freely, his hurting muscles relaxing slightly, he climbed into the saddle, took the reins and jabbed his heels.

'Now I'm in real trouble,' he muttered, notionally riding north for Little Missouri Valley.

3

Three months almost to the day after he had escaped from Fort Clinton, it was a different Ruben Byrd who rode Growler Ridge towards the town of Quinnel. Laying up on the dodge in one-horse towns had dulled his morale again. It was midsummer, the War had now been over for two months and the Volunteer Militia had disbanded. But nothing was ended for Ruben. He was wanted to answer charges, and it wasn't only the military who sought him. A pair of ex-officers from the Volunteers were on his trail because a £1,000 bounty had been put on his head, dead or alive. And the men had a second consideration: to avenge the dead that were left on the battlefield at Jonesboro.

Similarly, Ruben was doing his own hunting. Somewhere in Arkansas, two men were living on the proceeds of treachery. They were able to live a comfortable, untroubled life because after his escape from Fort Clinton, Ruben became the wanted, not them. He had to stay free to clear his name, and that meant finding them, and possibly killing them, and his vitals cramped at the thought.

* * *

The afternoon sun was dipping low as Ruben rode the long ridge. Below, and to the east, Quinnel was huddled on the banks of Strawberry River. Even in the soft light it stood stark and uninviting. An end township, it owed its existence to the Butterfield Stage, and a freighter train connecting with the boat yards at Memphis, Tennessee. He hauled on the reins, dug into his vest and pulled out his Brown Mule. He bit deep into the plug and tore off a chunk, chewed easily as he eyed the land.

'We'll wait till it gets dark,' he muttered. Both of them were tired and the roan whinnied and pawed at the flinty ground.

Ruben slipped from the saddle and walked to a rocky knuckle. He hunkered down, watched a ribbon of spiralling dust as the afternoon stagecoach rolled its way south towards Newport and Little Rock.

Since fleeing from the military he had drifted to the lurking holes, staying clear of towns and settlements. He had taken work wherever he could find it, keeping to himself, making enough dollars to equip himself with a decent horse, saddle and second-hand .36 Navy Colt. When anyone started asking questions he drifted on. Only once was he nearly caught. On a ranch outside of Yellville, a one-time Volunteer was working as a horse wrangler. For a few days the man had watched him, trying to recall where he'd seen him before. Ruben heard him discussing it with a bunkmate, knew the realization of a matched name and face was only a short time away. That meant another flight, and leaving his traps which he'd reflected ironically, were mostly stolen in the first place.

As the sun dipped below the horizon and twilight spread over the town, Ruben remounted, slowly descended the northern slope of the ridge. Holding his mackinaw jacket to his chest, he hunched in the saddle against the breeze that was blowing direct from the Ozark Plateau. Though he had learned to relax some, his face still carried the mien of resentment, the sharp penetrating stare, which most people shied away from. In a short period of time, he'd become a loner, a man without roots or friends.

'When I get rid of the enemy, I'll have me a full deck,' he frequently reminded himself.

★   ★   ★

Quinnel's main street was crowded when Ruben rode in. Oil lights suspended from poles cast sickly yellowish light, emphasizing the starkness of the town. He kept to the side of the street, his eyes darting about him, uneasy of anyone who passed. He half-expected someone to shout his name, the sudden blow of discovery. Gripping the reins tighter, he walked the roan on towards the middle of town, checking involuntarily when he saw the overhanging sign of the sheriff's office. His action surprised the roan and it crow-hopped a couple of steps. Two men on the boardwalk turned their heads towards him, but after a half-interested glance, returned to their conversation. As though summoned by the crooked finger of an unseen hand. Ruben reined in and dismounted. He crossed the boardwalk and steeled himself to approach the notice board outside of the darkened law office.

What he thought he might see, he did. Among the civic warnings and notifications, were three circulars, and one listed him. One thousand dollars dead or alive, was the caption. In a supporting column, was his description and the crimes. Fortunately, the copy had been prepared by someone with little concern for reliability or truthfulness. The portrayal was so broad it could have fitted half the men in Arkansas.

Ruben sighed with short-term relief, nearly smiled. *They'll have to know me, so I'll probably know them*, he thought. *And that most likely means Volunteers.* Many had known and rode with him before the bloodbath at Jonesboro, and for three weeks at Fort Clinton, many more had made it their business to seek him out. A traitor was a rare thing, and they were curious to know what one looked like.

Five minutes later, he reached the more lively part of town. On one side of the street was a bordello and a dog hole bar, and opposite was a suitable, busy-looking saloon. He headed the roan to the hitch rail. With deliberate movements he tied the reins, dusted himself and casually stepped to the boardwalk. The establishment sounded like it was well patronized, so, pulling down the front brim of his hat, he pushed through the bat wings.

Hanging from the ceiling were clusters of oil lamps which illuminated the big, single room. He let his eyes rove casually over the crowd, blinking against low curling smoke, raw aromas of the tobacco and stale beer. Satisfied he hadn't taken anyone's notice, he walked to the bar and asked for a glass of rye. He swallowed the spirit in one gulp, gave a slight cough as the trail dust washed free. He called for another, then leaned forward, looking at the bottles along the back bar.

'Lookin' for somethin' in particular?' the barman asked.

'Got anything with a label on it?'

The barman shook his head. 'Not much call,' he said. 'Passin' through?'

Keep civil, Ruben was thinking, *and calm*. The man just looked friendly, not intrusive.

'Yeah, that's right,' he replied. 'In one

end, out the other.'

'Ain't much work around here,' the barman continued. 'This town would peg out if it weren't for the bull trains an' John Butterfield.'

Ruben thought that if he was passing through, he wouldn't be looking for work. But he didn't say so and the man continued.

'Ranches in these parts are goin' through a lean ol' time ... shirt-tail outfits mostly. They lost their stock during the war. Had it requisitioned, or appropriated one way or another. Left 'em with nothin' to breed from, though.'

Ruben spilled some coins on the gleaming, wet counter. He wasn't much good at small talk. Over the past four months he'd got used to the idea of being left alone, making his own company. When the barman was called to the far end of the bar, he sighed with relief, straightened and drained the whiskey. Then he decided he could probably manage one more before riding on.

He looked down at the change on the bar, added a few more cents. As he pushed the small pile together, he looked up into the long mirror. The sporting girls had found customers and the tables were full. Behind them, the dice and Spanish monte tables were in full swing, bankers skilfully operating while watching the clientele at the same time.

Ruben watched for a few moments, then he felt the icy bite between his shoulder blades, stared in astonishment at the mirrored image. Near the front, nearest row of tables, a man was poised motionless. He was standing with set shoulders and his eyes were fixed on Ruben. For the shortest moment their eyes met, then the man made a quick grab for his gun.

Ruben's reaction was instant and he threw himself sideways. His Colt was already in his hand, thumb setting the action, firing as he turned.

There was an almost simultaneous

crash of gunfire, and the stranger's bullet ploughed across the top of the bar. It went over Ruben's head, sending shards of splintered glass flying.

On joining the Volunteer Militia, Ruben had received a hasty lesson in engaging with the enemy.

'Remember, if you get in a fight, it's usually who's *first*, not *best*, who gets to walk away,' his platoon corporal had advised.

Now, Ruben had heeded that advice. And his aim was better.

The assailant grimaced with surprise and pain, bent forward and staggered backwards. He dropped his revolver, used both hands to grasp his stomach as his legs gave way.

'Don't matter if it's battleground or bar. An' go for the belly. It's the biggest target,' the Arkansas corporal had also said.

Ruben got that right too.

The general clamour was suddenly quietened, a spike in the customers' interest. But a saloon shooting was as customary as daybreak, and moments later the customers went back to their drinks, cards or women, the incident all but forgotten.

One man ran for the sheriff, while at the bar, the barman was soaking up the spillage and scraping up the breakages. For the benefit of one or two others who'd had their backs turned, he was telling the story as he'd seen it.

The eyes of the prospective back-shooter were staring straight up at the oil lamps when Ruben knelt beside him.

'Do you know me, feller?' Ruben asked, not recalling having seen the man before.

The man blinked, shifted his frightened eyes. 'You're Ruben Byrd,' he gasped. 'I thought you was after me.'

'Why would Ruben Byrd be after you?'

'There's reasons. How bad am I?'

Ruben looked down at the blood oozing across the man's fingers, spreading across his shirt.

'I was going for as bad as it gets,' he said. 'It was your mistake.'

The man came up with an agonizing cough and bright blood appeared between his lips. 'One of 'em,' he spluttered. 'I let Fornell talk me into it . . . damn him.'

'Who's Fornell? Who are you?' Ruben demanded.

'John McSwane. Me an' Lester Fornell sold out to Buckley. When we heard you were taken to Fort Clinton, we thought we were clear. You goin' to get me a doc?'

'Yeah, of course. I need you alive,' Ruben said.

'That's good. Thanks.'

Ruben considered the consequences of catching one of the traitors. *It's the answer . . . the way out*, he thought. 'You thought I was after you?'

McSwane tried to move himself, decided the pain was too much. 'I'm not goin' to live.'

'You are. I promise. Just keep talking.'

'It was Fornell's idea. He'd had enough o' the fightin' . . . wanted out, jus' like the rest of us,' McSwane continued. 'But he wasn't goin' empty-handed . . . reckoned he was owed somethin'. He heard the Runners were offerin' big money for information. Hell, we all knew that. Some o' them boys were as good as kin.'

McSwane didn't seem to be much beyond his majority. His chin was hardly whiskered under the blood now spilling more quickly from his mouth.

Ruben looked thoughtful, thought the man was near finished. 'Where do I find Fornell?' he asked.

'It was his idea. He forced me to go on with him.'

'Yeah, I know that,' Ruben said impatiently. 'And it's a bit late for trying to absolve yourself. Tell me where he is, goddamnit.'

'Vinegar Wells. He's in Vinegar Wells. Everyone thought he was dead.'

'What else?'

'It was him who got the money

. . . not me. He said to keep my mouth shut. Then he was gone. I've seen him just the once.'

'How did you know about me?' Ruben asked.

'From the Fort. I thought you were on to me.' McSwane's eyes moved slowly as he lifted his bloody hand. 'I don't want to die, Byrd. Not now I'm safe.'

'You're not safe, you miserable son-of-a-bitch. You're dying. And you're not going to live long enough to tell anyone what I need you to, goddamnit.'

'You said someone's on their way.'

'They are, but don't stop now. What's Fornell look like?'

'He'll shoot me dead, if I say anythin'.'

'No, he won't. Tell me about him.'

McSwane took a short, gurgled breath and closed his eyes. 'Where's that sawbones? I'm hurtin' bad.' He stopped and more blood spewed from his mouth. 'Lester Fornell . . . he ain't what . . . '

For a few moments. Ruben refused

to accept that McSwane had died. He wanted to shake the man back to life until the sheriff arrived. Now I've got to start over, he thought. *And it was me who killed you*. He cursed under his breath, was about to start searching through McSwane's pockets when he heard the upsurge of noise from outside the saloon.

'Where are they?' a strident voice called.

'In there,' came the reply.

Taking a guess at who was approaching, Ruben got to his feet and backed off. He looked behind him, located a rear door that would lead to the office and store rooms of the saloon. He caught the barman's eye, gave him the look that said, don't do anything that would risk my wellbeing.

'Is he dead?' the sheriff asked on coming through the swing doors.

The barman was walking towards the body of McSwane. 'Haven't had time to check. But by the look of him, I'd say yes,' he replied.

'Where's the feller who shot him?'

'He raced out. I'd say beyond town limits by now. But before you go chasin' him, Sheriff, it was this feller here who started it. He was gettin' set for a back-shoot. I saw it all.'

The sheriff looked up from the body, directly into the face of the barman, 'So why's he made a run for it?'

At the rear of the saloon, screened by a heavy drape, Ruben was holding his breath. He stood unmoving with his back against the rear wall of the saloon, his Colt held across his chest. He couldn't let himself be discovered, or give himself up. When it came out who he was, he wouldn't stand a chance. Somehow, he had to get to his horse. But with townsfolk now congregating on the boardwalks outside, that seemed unlikely.

'Was he a stranger?' the sheriff asked.

'They both are,' the barman replied. 'I've not seen either of 'em before.'

'I've seen the croaker,' another voice broke in. 'He's been around a week or

49

so. Always on his own.'

'He certainly never drank here,' the barman added.

'Well there's somethin' between 'em. Or was,' the sheriff growled. He delved into McSwane's pockets and withdrew some folded papers. 'Travel documents. Letter of passage or the like? Looks like he was from the Volunteer Militia. Name o' McSwane . . . John D. McSwane.'

'Never heard of him,' the barman said, and a few others shook their heads in accord.

'Well, unless I'm mistaken, an' I ain't usually, there's a true bill out on him. Him or the other one. They're wanted for bein' a double agent, an' there's a big reward. I can't recall his name right now.'

'Me neither. But I saw the notice,' the barman added. 'If this is him, the other feller might have been on his trail.'

'No, it don't figure.' The sheriff stood up and shoved the papers inside his coat. 'He'd have been military. An' if he had been, he'd have stopped. Maybe even paid his compliments. Besides, if our dead friend here's on leg bail, why'd he hang around for a week? I reckon it's the other way round.'

Ruben grimaced as the sheriff reached his conclusion. His first thought was how many of the saloon's clientele would react to the notion of a big reward. He imagined them pointing, nodding in his direction. But in Ruben's experience, not a lot of folk would help a sheriff in a similar situation. There were usually safety issues, and it wasn't what they got paid for. But if he stayed where he was, there was a chance he'd soon find out how much sway $1,000 carried.

He had to take a risk. With his left hand, he reached behind him and eased open the rear, side door. He poked his head out, saw a handful of men milling around where the side alley met with the main street, the corner of the saloon. *Both escape options open*, he thought wryly. So he cursed them all quietly and stepped into the alley, walked confidently towards them.

With their fearful concentration on the saloon doors, the men didn't pay Ruben much heed. They had no idea who he was, probably thought he was one of them gone for a leak. As he walked around them for the hitch rail, he fought the impulse to hurry. He was waiting for one of them to recognize him, call for the lawman, shout for him to stop. Anything to initiate a wild flight from town.

Though it only took a few seconds, it felt an interminable length of time to reach his horse. With trembling fingers he unwound the reins from the hitch rail, deciding that if any one of them should so much as look twice at him, he'd shoot up the boardwalk. Stepping up into the saddle, he took a deep breath, turned the mount's head for the north end of town.

From the saloon doors, the barman stared hard at Ruben's back.

'He's gettin' away,' he yelled. 'He was

here all the time. Goddamn squealer must've heard us put the finger on him.' The barman had been fully aware of Ruben's silent presence in the saloon. But he'd had the warning, didn't want to be the one catching a bullet.

Ruben dug his heels into the roan's flanks, urging it to a gallop. 'Run for it,' he yelled. 'This time I know where we're going.'

From the boardwalk the sheriff gave a dutiful demand for Ruben to stop. Then he pulled a long-barrelled Colt, took careful aim and pulled the trigger.

But Ruben was too far down the street, it was too dark and he was a moving target. One man stepped away from the group and raised a rifle, decided an effective shot wasn't on.

Ruben ran on to the edge of town, then swung west. Behind him the sheriff was now speaking to the people gathering around him.

'If any o' you want a slice o' that reward, you can saddle up right now an' earn it,' he told them. 'An' someone sort out that body in the saloon. It ain't goin' to get any sweeter.'

* * *

Ruben kept the roan at full gallop. He was heading back to the place where he'd first looked on Quinnel, from Growler Ridge. He turned in the saddle, couldn't see much, but guessed the posse with the sheriff taking point would be no more than a mile behind. He decided to swing away from the trail, racing towards where he saw the broad gleaming ribbon that was Strawberry River. But in the moonlight, his turn was seen by the following riders who swept around to try and cut him off.

Ruben made it to the river flats and galloped his mount straight into the river. The water was deeper than he'd anticipated, and he was thrown from the saddle as the roan lost its footing. But the current wasn't strong, and he pulled the horse's head around, facing it towards the opposite bank.

'Spread an' listen for him,' the sheriff called out, his words cutting through the otherwise silent darkness.

As Ruben made it to the opposite bank, he heard the dash and splatter of the posse as they entered the water behind him. Ten yards downriver he saw the shape of a big old willow with roots scoured from the rush of many winters' high water. Under cover of the surrounding darkness he swam the horse towards it. He was breathing heavy as he forced himself and the roan around and in between the tangle of root and low, hanging branches. Bending into the roan's neck, he waited, the chill of the water and fear of cotton-mouths making him shudder.

'Can you see him?' the sheriff called.

'No. Don't see how he could be here,' a voice answered. 'I reckon he's gone downstream.'

'Stay on that side, an' watch the bank. Keep low. You'll see him against skyline if he rides out. We'll ride on, see if there's any sign.'

Ruben hardly dared to breathe as some of the posse rode past where he was screened by the gnarled old willow. He leaned further to one side, looked into the black lustrous eye of his horse and stroked its head. 'You're doing good,' he whispered. 'We both are.'

He shuddered again at the sound of hoofs digging in and out of the mud at the side of the river. They sounded so close, he thought he could put out his hand and touch them. Three riders passed by. He sat waiting for many minutes until there was no further sound and he dared move. He carefully worked his way from under the willow, slid from the saddle and led the horse from the water.

As the roan shook itself, Ruben pulled off his boots. He emptied them of water, quickly put them back on before he couldn't. He felt in his pockets and drew out a few sodden dollar notes and tobacco. Then he patted his bedroll, wondered about his spare clothing and camp trappings in his saddlebags. He looked up as a blanket of cloud moved across the moon. He wanted the advantage of the deeper darkness and climbed back into the saddle.

'We'll all meet at Vinegar Wells,' he said. 'Let's go.'

4

The night was dark and low flames danced across the firewood. Ruben placed the small battered pan into the heat, poked around at the strips of fatty bacon. He watched the sizzle, chewing appreciatively on the last of his plug tobacco. Minutes later he tipped in some beans, mixing them around the glistening fat. From one of his saddle-bags he unwrapped a piece of stale bread, grinned and added it to the pan. The coffee had boiled and was sitting in the mound of ash.

He was high in the hills, two miles west of Vinegar Wells. As he ate, he peered down at the pin-pricks of light that patterned the town. His months on the run had taught him to seek the highest ground possible, get a broad, clear view of the neighbouring land. If he was going to be caught it wouldn't be through surprise or carelessness. As he chewed on the fried bread and bacon, he recalled the way he'd seen the town when he'd reached his position before first dark the previous afternoon.

The town was more substantial than Quinnel. There were many more buildings, orderly and painted, some of them brick. Order seemed to be an important concern for the town. Four streets ran at right-angles from the main street that was lined with elder. In the centre of the town a giant cottonwood shaded stone seats. A stretch of the Bitter River, curled in a loop around the outskirts. It created a natural line of defence, at the same time leaving a break for the spur line that linked with the railhead at St Louis. Ruben was impressed by the arrangement. But now as he lay in the rough ground above the town, his thoughts turned once again to his exchange with John McSwane.

Somewhere not too far away, there

was a man who could clear him. He had a name, but would it be enough? There was something that McSwane was going to tell him, but didn't get around to. *What the hell was it*, he wondered.

He sat up, looked thoughtfully at the flickering lights of the town. 'He ain't . . . ' were McSwane's dying words. But what did it mean? That Fornell wasn't going to give up without a fight? That he ain't got no shame . . . no heart . . . no legs? Hell, what was it he was going to say? Ruben tried to imagine himself in Lester Fornell's position. Logically, where should he start to look?

He cleaned up his eating gear, stowed it in a saddle-bag and built up the fire. He wondered if his quarry spent much time looking around him, if he was somewhere down there now, looking to the hills. After spreading his bedroll, he went to check on the roan, walking it close to a trickle of spring water before securing the hobbles.

Within ten minutes of placing his head on his saddle he was into a restless sleep.

The first rays of morning light stirred him, got him to his feet. Before the sun had time to reach the rim of the hills, he saddled the roan and headed for the town trail.

As he rode he felt his body tensing, the turmoil of not knowing, creeping into his vitals. Perhaps the sheriff of Quinnel had sent out a wire that he was around. For all he knew, the sheriff would be sitting outside his office waiting for him. But he knew that was unlikely, nothing more than an acceptable risk he had to take. All he had to do was get to Fornell before the law got to him.

Beyond the slope of the foothills, he rode past a group of cowhands working on what looked like boundary fencing. He returned their friendly gestures with a polite nod. He didn't want to bring attention to himself, pondering on their likely reaction if they had known who he was and what he was doing there. So, best not ask them if they knew the whereabouts of a Lester Fornell, he decided.

His opinion of Vinegar Wells didn't change as he rode into the town's main street. Though it was still quite deserted, he could see that civic pride manifested itself early. The litter and debris from the previous day had been swept into piles at the corner of each street. At the far end, a low-sided cart was being pulled slow and determinedly by a grey, pudding foot mare. In front, two men with large shovels were collecting the rubbish.

Ruben looked down at his threadbare trousers. *You might be wielding shovels, but you both got the outfit edge,* he thought. All of his clothing was shabby, his boots caked with mud and dust. He rubbed a self-conscious hand over the stubble on his chin, looked at a brightly painted, two-storey building named Town Palace. A swinging sign read: *Room and Board at reasonable prices.*

No troublemakers.

Brushing the front of his shirt in an illusory attempt to make himself presentable, he led the roan to the line of iron hitching posts. As he was untying his saddle-bags, he reciprocated when a couple of townsfolk looked his way, bid him a tentative good morning.

Behind the hotel's desk, a clerk who was riffling a sheaf of papers took time looking up when Ruben entered. 'Good morning. Something we can do for you?' the man's voice inquired, as though there must be something he couldn't think of.

'I'd like a room and use of a bath,' Ruben said. 'And someone to organize water, hay and a handful of oats for my partner. He's waiting outside.'

The clerk took a deep breath, looked Ruben up and down. 'The sign outside says no troublemakers. That includes wiseacres.'

Ruben swung his saddle-bags across the counter, and dug into a pocket of his trousers. He snapped two silver dollars down on the desk top.

'I'm neither of those things, or illiterate,' he said coolly. 'Have you got somewhere or not?' He wanted to say a lot more, but he knew he couldn't risk the consequences.

The clerk sniffed unhappily but passed the key over. A minute later, he called for the hotel stableman to take Ruben's horse to the stable out back.

Upstairs, Ruben wasted no time in taking his bath, smoothing out his alternative clothing. Meantime, the clerk had taken a good look at the name in the register. Then, he too wasted no time, walking hurriedly from the hotel to the sheriff's office.

Knowledge of any newcomer was the way George Jasper wanted it. The sheriff of Vinegar Wells made it his business to know who and what was in town. It was his way of laying trouble, being one step ahead.

Ruben had finished his sprucing up, and as he stowed his dirty gear in a saddle-bag he suddenly felt hungry. He stood looking out of the window, noted the clear boardwalks, that the piles of rubbish had been removed. He wondered if anyone had ever thought of pulling a breakfast wagon up and down the street. Offering steak, eggs and coffee, there was a small fortune to be made. A chuck wagon for town folk, he thought. Then he recalled where he'd seen the establishment he was thinking of. It was out by the corrals as he rode in — a low, adobe eatery whose board proclaimed you could fill your paunch twice over for one full dollar.

Ruben walked down the stairs to the hotel's lobby area, looking resolutely ahead, away from where he thought the clerk might be at the desk. He stepped out to the boardwalk, was about to cross the street, when a voice called out.

'Hold it there, Ruben. Don't move your hands. Just stand still.'

Ruben did as he was told. He knew

who it was. He recognized the voice from years back in his past, and cursed his bad luck.

* * *

Ruben sipped his coffee, looked across the desk to where George Jasper was eyeing him keenly. In front of him, his Colt and gun-belt were atop a short stack of wanted dodgers.

'I always take a look at strangers, soon as they ride into town,' Jasper explained. 'There's one or two folk know that's the way I like it. Hah, I sure didn't expect to run into my ol' pard. You was just plumb unlucky.' The sheriff sounded amenable enough, but his steely eyes met Ruben's without a flicker.

Ruben smiled wryly. 'The same kind o' luck that put me outside the law, George.'

'I never figured you'd show in Vinegar Wells. Did you know I was here?'

66

'No. I've not heard of you since before the War.'

Jasper drummed his fingers on the desk. 'There's been a lot o' water along a lot o' rivers since then, Rube. But it don't make a difference. You an' me go back a long way.'

'You always were some sort of lawman, George. I don't see why the two shouldn't be mutual. What are you going to do?'

Jasper got up from his chair, moved closer to sit on the edge of the desk. For a long moment he looked hard at Ruben. 'Depends,' he said. 'What was it brought you here . . . to Vinegar Wells?'

Ruben slowly placed the coffee mug on the desk, sat back as if to counter Jasper's move.

'You heard from Quinnel lately?' he asked in return.

In reply, Jasper opened a drawer beside him. He pulled out and unfolded a telegraph form, handed it to Ruben.

Ruben read it and nodded. 'Yeah, that was me all right, and just like it says. McSwane tried a backshoot on me.'

'So what stopped him?'

'Me. I saw him in the mirror. It was him who gave intelligence to General Bluebelly. He thought I'd found out who he was, and that I was after him.'

Jasper's expression remained impassive. 'How'd you know all this?'

'He told me before he died. The son-of-a-bitch thought it would save him.'

Jasper's manner was still cold and searching. 'There's a dodger says you shot him because he was after you. That he recognized you as the turncoat. How's anyone supposed to know who or what to believe, Rube?'

Ruben shook his head. He knew it would be this way. What proof did he have, now that McSwane was dead? 'If you don't know, George, it's little use me telling you,' he replied sadly. 'McSwane told me the other man was named Lester Fornell, that he was in Vinegar Wells. He's here in your town

. . . the town you like to keep a lid on.'

'There's no one called Fornell here,' Jasper replied. 'I reckon your story must have a kink in it somewhere.'

Ruben's hands gripped the chair and he returned the sheriff's searching look. 'Is that your way of calling me a liar, George?'

'Hell no, I believe you. Beginnin' to, anyway,' Jasper said, moving off the edge of the desk. 'I didn't say you were lying. I said there must be somethin' wrong with your story. There's a difference. You add it up, Rube. Four months or more you've been on the owl hoot with every goddamn lawman west o' the Mississippi wantin' your hide. Them an' half the old Confederate Army. Now, you shoot a man down, outrun a posse, an' come here with a story you can't back up. If you was me, what would you do, right now?'

'Well, if you believe me, why not go with my story? It fits as well as any other.' Ruben eased himself from the chair and started pacing the jail office.

69

'Either that or arrest me,' he muttered. 'And come to the hanging. Think, George. You can watch my last jig, still believing in me. Hell, what a story for the gran'children.'

Jasper's eyes narrowed as he considered Ruben's words.

'Did I ever lie to you, George?' Ruben continued. 'You ever know me to lie to anyone?'

Jasper lowered his head and surveyed his boots. His face was screwed into a deep frown. 'No. Your pa would've skinned you, same as mine would've me. Hell, Ruben, why'd you ride into my town?'

'Because Fornell's here. Let me go get him.'

Jasper raised his eyes. 'You're askin' a hell of a lot, Rube. If I was to let go every bonehead who wants to prove 'emselves . . . '

'I'm not every bonehead for chris'sakes. Who the hell's going to know? If I take a powder, keep quiet. If I catch up with Fornell, I'll say it was down to you. Your wise dispensing of law and justice. Come on, George. For months I've been running around in circles. Now I've got a lead. What do you say?'

Jasper walked back to his chair, flopped down and stared round his jail. 'Yeah, use old instincts instead of trying to match up old dodgers,' he said. He looked at the sheaf of papers on his desk, closed his eyes for a moment, thoughtfully. 'OK, Rube, you tell me what happened . . . all of it. Don't leave stuff out.'

★   ★   ★

Ruben started from the time he lay in a muddy hollow outside Jonesboro. He told of the arrival of Buckley's Runners, his battle to rejoin the troop and of his captivity in Fort Clinton. He grinned impassively as he related his escape. 'I never did get to hear what happened to the guard.'

'You should, it was you who did it,'

Jasper snorted. 'You broke his jaw an' a couple o' ribs.'

'On behalf of other inmates, I should have done better. He was one of the thugs who ran a regular stampede over me. So, when I got out, I vamoosed. I had no idea of what to do or where to go, other than make for the high ground.'

'What took you to Quinnel?'

Ruben shrugged. 'Nothing in particular. Like I said, I was on the move.'

'An' you'd never seen McSwane before?'

'No, not to my knowledge.'

Jasper lifted a boot heel to the desk top in front of him. His eyes were steely again, but more considerate as he listened to Ruben continue.

'First time I laid eyes on him was in the back bar mirror of the saloon.'

'I know what happened next. You say before he died he told you he was one of the two men? The ones givin' information to the enemy?'

'Yeah, that's right. I let him think I'd

get the doc for him if he coughed up.'

'Hmm. He could have been your partner an' you double-crossed him,' Jasper offered. 'An' before you get crusty again, I'm only lookin' at the options . . . like others will.'

'You think what you've said's a possibility?'

'Not really. Having killed you, he'd have had the same problem you've got now.'

'So why say it?'

'I'm the only man who can give you a chance to prove yourself, Rube. But in doin' it, I'm puttin' my job on the line. I want to know exactly where I stand. You can see that, can't you?'

'Right now, it's hard to see anything other than my own predicament.' Ruben carried on with the story, his voice slightly edgy. When he'd finished, Jasper reached for Ruben's clasp knife.

'Put this back in your pocket,' he said with a stiff smile. 'I guess if I'd been McSwane, I'd have tried to bushwhack you. Specially having had this Fornell cove as a partner. An' there's no one o' that name in this town, Rube. Never has been.'

There was a long moment's silence before Ruben responded. 'Hell, that was it,' he exclaimed. 'It's so goddamn obvious.'

'What is? What are you talkin' about?'

'What McSwane was going to tell me. He was going to say that Fornell wasn't using his real name. I've been thinking it was something to do with him riding on . . . going someplace else, but it wasn't. He is in this town, George. He's just not calling himself Lester Fornell.'

'Yeah. It's what he might do, I guess. It's one hell of a risk, waitin' for the past to catch up.'

'Are you still looking at those options, George?'

'I'll always be doing that, Rube. Always a lawman. What's important right now is findin' out if McSwane told you the truth. So, I'm leanin' your way for forty-eight hours. Unless you come up with somethin', I'll take you in. It ain't reasonable to expect less o' me. You know it.' Jasper determined. 'An' I want your word that you won't return to the high ground.'

Ruben frowned, nodded his acceptance of the ultimatum. 'Fair enough. Forty-eight hours doesn't exactly give me much time.'

'It's time enough for my neck to be stuck out,' Jasper replied quickly. 'Now, when's this Fornell . . . or whatever he's callin' himself, supposed to have rode in here?'

'I don't know. That is, I'm not sure. He might even have arrived on the train. But it would have been in the last six months. Who've you got?'

Jasper made thinking sounds, closing his eyes as he thought back. 'There's been three newcomers I can recall. Drifters stay a week at most, usually less.'

Ruben felt immediate frustration. What if Fornell had been one of them?

He wouldn't have a hope. Worse, he'd lose his freedom, probably his life due to the promise with Jasper. *Yeah, well, I could break that*, he thought.

Jasper continued. 'The first o' the three's Drew Desmond. He had a wife, but I can't think why . . . why she stuck to him. He had a mistress called a faro table. You don't get a real day's work in by livin' at the saloon.'

'Had, you say?'

'Yeah, he's dead. Caught a bullet a few weeks ago.'

'Who by?'

'It's an open case, an' not exactly a priority.'

'Who's suspected?'

'The sort he gambled with? Could've been one o' many. Hell, he was a cardsharp. A goddamn lucky one.'

'Doesn't stop it running out,' Ruben muttered, but not enough to stop Jasper.

'When him an' his missus arrived, they were broke . . . didn't have a pot to piss in. But inside a month he'd turned enough to put down on a decent-lookin' house.'

'Was he a cheat?'

Jasper shook his head. 'Never heard it actually said. Must've been some punters who thought it, though. Maybe one in particular.'

'He doesn't sound like my man.'

'But he could have been, if you get my meanin',' Jasper suggested, his voice lowering. 'If he was . . . '

Ruben nodded to show he understood the implication, although he wasn't certain he did.

'Then there's the other feller,' Jasper said. 'A no account low life by the name of Travis Apling. He tried his hand at every crime you can think of . . . no doubt some you couldn't. So I wouldn't be surprised if double-dealing an' betrayal, figured.'

'Where do I find him?'

'In the Boot Hill cemetery. We hung him ten days ago for murder.'

'Jesus,' Ruben cursed. 'What the hell are you giving me here, George? A brace of dead men? Is this your sheriff trick to get me in the jailhouse? How the hell do I clear myself if everyone's dead?'

'It ain't my fault, Rube. Perhaps it's because they're all more or less in the same business. You asked who I've got, I'm tellin' you.'

Ruben gave the sheriff an irritated glare. 'You said three. So, that leaves us with the prize turkey. Unless he's got grass waving over him, too.'

'This one's alive an' kickin'. His name's Fergus Stearne, an' he owns the Applejack Room, along the street. Unlike the Fromes, he arrived with stake money. Made it from riverboat trade on the Big Muddy, apparently. That'd be seven or eight months ago. But I can't see him bein' your man. He's well regarded around here.'

'When you say 'around here', does that include you, George?'

'I guess. It ain't a troublesome saloon.'

'Roy Bean was well regarded and he

didn't have that sort of trouble either. And for all the wrong reasons,' Ruben returned drily.

Jasper gave a strained smile, then continued. 'Must admit I don't know much else about him,' he conceded. 'From his manner an' speech, I'd say he's Arkansan. But certainly no hillbilly. He keeps a good house, no brawlin' or funny business. His girls are clean, his liquor's good, an' he's earned respect in the short time he's been here.

'I can't see him bein' anythin' other than what he is.'

'I understand that, George. But if all bad folk looked and sounded like bad folk, we could pick 'em out, couldn't we? Lawmen wouldn't have to go looking for 'em. If he's so accomplished and personable, do you think he could be acting his way through all this. New town . . . new production . . . new part?'

Staring hard into Ruben's face, Jasper took his feet off the desk. 'I hadn't thought about that, no. But then the same applies to you, Rube . . . all of us. Difference bein', you're the one in trouble.'

Ruben dipped his head like a bull considering a charge. 'Touché,' he said.

'Now you more understand my position, don't let me down,' Jasper warned. 'I'll help you if I can. But turn me over, an' there's a side you ain't too familiar with — one you won't want to go up against. Now where were we?'

'Just about to shake hands, I think. You said Desmond's widow is still in town?'

'Not at the moment. She had his body shipped to a family plot near the Beaver Lakes. Seems he actually was a wrong'un . . . the proverbial black sheep. I guess she'll be back sometime soon.'

'She might know something. Unless it's very soon, it doesn't really matter.'

'I don't think it would, anyway,' Jasper said. 'And as for Travis Apling, he'd never have been your man. He was on the owl hoot long before the War started. Nearest he got to any army was when he made the mistake of holdin' up one o' their relief wagons. Arms is one thing, but he took their beef meat.'

Ruben got to his feet and set his hat firmly. He looked at the cells and smiled. 'I hope those bunks are comfortable. The way things are stacked, I might be making their acquaintance.'

'We'll think about that forty-eight hours from now.'

Ruben walked to the door and paused. 'There's just a couple more things, George. You say Stearne brought in cash?'

'Yeah, enough seed to get himself well set up. But that don't necessarily mean anything. For someone who's made some money, an end o' the line town's a profitable venture . . . ripe for development. Cash goes a hell of a long way out here. A lot further than the big cities. Anythin' else?'

'You can give me my Colt back.'

Jasper nodded and picked up

Ruben's Colt. 'If you have to use it, be real careful,' he advised, handing it over. 'Is that it?'

'Not quite. It's about who I am.'

'Don't worry about that. Folk around here don't know about you. An' you've not exactly met many of 'em. Besides, in this neck o' the woods, short memories are useful.'

'What about the hotel clerk? I've met him.'

'He knows nothin' more than what he told me, an' that's the way it'll stay. Like I said, Rube, don't worry.'

Ruben gave a considerate nod, opened the door and stepped on to the boardwalk.

'Are you headin' for the Applejack?' Jasper called out.

'I thought I might. It's a start.'

'Yeah, of what? You get into any scrapes an' that forty-eight hours goes up in smoke, an' you along with it. Take heed, Rube,' Jasper cautioned.

5

The Applejack Room was as the sheriff had described it. It was one of the calmest, most peaceable saloons Ruben had ever seen, a place to be impressed by. Once through the heavy, ornate swing doors, there was an immediate and enveloping sense of cosiness. Mostly it was from the decoration, the deep red of plush seats and papered walls. Underfoot, the boards were scrubbed, without sawdust. The tables were shining, and to Ruben's amazement were provided with ashtrays and cuspidors. The bar was sparkling bright, the full-length mirror reflecting rows of labelled, McCoy liquor. He looked up to the massive, glass chandelier that hung from an iron boss in the centre of the room. The paintwork of the ceiling was scrubbed to allay the dark, treacly residues from pipe and tobacco smoke.

The staircase, running in a broad curve to the gallery, was carpeted in the same deep red of the drapes that screened the rooms above. The girls weren't around yet. Ruben thought it a bit early for their more stimulating contribution.

Self-consciously, he walked to the bar, digging for a silver dollar as he approached. He realized his gaffe, nodded unassumingly as the barman moved up to serve him. He noticed that the outfits of some of the standing drinkers didn't reflect the setting. Generally dust-caked, they looked like dried up cowboys who were admiring the decorative sights. Ruben guessed they were too intimidated by their rich surroundings to be anything other than well-behaved. He took note of the faro game in the corner, that the only raised sound was that of the players' nervous participation.

'Howdy,' the barman greeted. 'Your pleasure?'

Ruben was tempted to agree, and leave it at that. 'Bourbon. Old Crow, if it's on hand,' he said.

The barman nodded, reached for a bottle behind him on the back bar. He filled the shot glass and pushed it towards Ruben, wiping the counter top with his cloth.

'Your first time here at the Applejack?' he inquired.

'Yeah. You were recommended,' Ruben answered. 'Looks like a real peaceable kind of place.'

'You could say that.' The barman gave an inscrutable smile. 'But then I've been here longer. Since the day we opened, in fact.'

'So, other than opening night, it's not always like this? So convivial?'

'No, of course not. What is it they say? Soberness conceals and drunkenness reveals?'

'Something like that. I'd put it down to the drink.'

'And those who peddle it,' the barman replied with a humourless smile. 'There was trouble not so long back ... ended up with a public hanging. You don't see that too often, nowadays.'

'No. Maybe it's why I heard mention of it. It didn't come with the recommendation, you understand,' Ruben said, with what he hoped was an encouraging smile. 'Feller had a curious name, didn't he? Apple, was it?'

'Apling. Travis Apling. He was nasty piece o' work who shot dead a harmless old rummy. Robbed him of his money an' his timepiece. Less than twenty dollars all in, the son-of-a-bitch.'

'Was he local, this Apling?' Ruben asked. 'I'm guessing his victim was.'

'He was a piker who slept indoors ... had a room at the end of town. Seems he'd been one step ahead of the law for years ... mistook Vinegar Wells as ripe for his wretched work. He certainly figured George Jasper wrong.' The barman smirked as he recalled the memory. 'He was tried an' hanged before you could bat an eyelid. Wrong-doin' an' wrong do'ers don't count for much where our

86

lawman's concerned.'

'Yeah, I know what you mean,' Ruben said. 'I got hauled down to the jail before I had time for breakfast,' he added casually. 'Seems my name's not a popular one around here.'

'Why's that, then? You Mr Bogeyman or something?'

As Ruben was about to reply, he saw the barman's attention drawn to someone he'd seen over his shoulder. Ruben half turned as the man approached.

'Hi, boss. I was just exchangin' local stuff with this gent here,' the barman said.

With the merest suggestion of a smile, the man held out a hand. 'Fergus Stearne,' he introduced himself. 'I own the Applejack. You new to Vinegar Wells? I haven't seen you in here before.'

'Name's Ruben Byrd, and I rode in this morning. I might stay on, though, if the town'll have me.'

'That applies to most of us, Mr Byrd. What was it you were saying to Harry about not being popular? Is it something I should know about? Purely for professional reasons, of course.'

Is it you? Ruben thought, feeling a roll of his gut. *Are You Lester Fornell?* He took a few fast, short breaths.

'Of course,' he said. 'Let's sit somewhere, and I'll tell you.'

The barman filled two fresh glasses as Stearne indicated a nearby table.

Stearne was as tall as Ruben, and beneath the dark, conservatively cut suit, clearly kept himself in shape. And it was obvious he possessed an engaging personality, easy to understand why he was readily accepted by the townsfolk.

'Your estimable sheriff sure means to douse any likely trouble,' Ruben said. 'Does he check out everyone when they arrive?'

'He sure does,' Stearne chuckled. 'And if they don't measure up, they're sent back to where they came from. He dispatched one feller to St Louis nailed inside a packing case. It seems he's given you the OK.'

'Yeah, seems that way. But he did have me figured for someone on a Wanted dodger.'

Stearne thought for a moment. 'There'll be more than one Byrd in Arkansas, I guess,' he mused.

'Yeah. And one of 'em deserted from the army as a traitor. Hah, not the sort of references you want to ride into a new town with.' As he spoke, Ruben kept his eyes fixed on Stearne.

The saloon owner made no response. His smile remained accepting and friendly. 'I did hear something about that,' he nodded. 'Were you in the army?'

'Nope,' Ruben lied. 'My two brothers were, though,' he lied again. 'I stayed behind to look after the ranch. We were supplying direct to the foundries and gunpowder mills at Nashville. Excepted action, they called it. When the War ended, the boys came home. I decided to see what had happened to the country.'

'A rancher? Well, if you do decide to stay on, you shouldn't have any trouble getting work. Something appropriate. I happen to know someone who's looking for a ramrod.'

Ruben didn't involve himself and the conversation drifted to gossip. Stearne filled him in on the town's way of life and the work of the neighbouring ranches, as did Harry the barman, when he stepped away from being busy with customers. Ruben guessed the man did more than ply drinks and wipe down the bar. He knew that most good men needed a keeper to stay good. Maybe Harry was a shareholder, as he'd been there from the saloon's opening. As the talk went on, Ruben was getting more discouraged. He couldn't see Fergus Stearne as an army double agent. But then realized that affability could be a qualification, recalled asking George Jasper if he knew what a spy looked like.

'Well, if you'll excuse me,' Stearne said after a while. 'That ramrod work I mentioned? Perhaps in a day or two I can arrange for you to meet the ranch boss.'

'I'd be obliged,' Ruben returned.

'Good. That Old Crow's a fine swallow. Have another on the house.'

Harry noticed Ruben's contemplation as Stearne walked away.

'Never leaves you, does it?' he said. 'The self-confidence. Must be an army thing.'

Ruben's jaw twitched. 'He didn't mention he was in the army.'

Harry shrugged. 'Yeah. He spoke about it once . . . briefly. I think it was the Militia.'

As Harry moved off to speak to another customer, Ruben sought out Stearne again. *Kind of curious not to mention it,* he thought, staring at the man's back. *But was it? Lester Fornell was the soldier, not Fergus Stearne.* Ruben went back over their conversation, trying to recall a clue, an indication. If Stearne was Fornell, then it was one hell of an act he was living out. It didn't matter, though. Ruben knew it was him.

Ruben turned his attention to the bar drinkers. Sporadic laughter and harmless joshing took place, but there was little sign of the raucous, undomesticated behaviour usually found in end of line saloons. George Jasper had certainly tamed the town, but Ruben was doubtful if suppressing natural high spirits was always such a good thing.

Standing back at the bar, he shook his head. 'Seems more like a Sunday meeting, than a saloon,' he said when Harry returned. 'I'll take a beer.'

'Wasn't always like this,' Harry replied, on seeing the look on Ruben's face. 'I've heard that before Jasper came here, the place got through tables an' chairs like piles o' matchwood. Had 'emselves a fair share o' gunfights too. Today it's two shootin's in the last six months. I guess it's the creep of civilization. That, an' the barrel o' Jasper's Colt.'

'Yeah, I think he mentioned two to

me. What was the other fight about?'
Jasper inquired.

'Drew Desmond, an' it wasn't a fight. He had a way about him, too. You'd think he owned this place, the time he spent here. He was the only man I know who riled the boss. Certainly the only one who got away with it for more'n a couple of hours. Can't say he's missed much.'

Ruben leaned forward on the bar, his interest stirred. 'So what was it all about?'

Harry tugged pensively at an ear lobe. 'Difficult to put a finger on it, an' I've tried,' he said. 'He arrived soon after Stearne moved in. One night they were playing cards and they quarrelled over something. That was when I heard Stearne talking about the army . . . during the card game.'

'Was this Desmond feller an army man?'

'Can't say.' Harry wiped the cloth across the bar top, as if clearing away their conversation. 'I do know he was one hell of a player. Him and the boss played regular once a week. Desmond nearly always won. Some say enough to live real high off the hog.'

'Could be Stearne's not that good,' Ruben suggested quietly.

Harry shook his head. 'There's the funny thing. He's one o' the best I ever saw. But not up against Desmond.'

'How'd he get shot?'

'No one knows. Well, someone does. It was a Friday night, out back of here, but we don't know why. Desmond was a tinhorn, but he didn't make enemies. None that would shoot him dead for a night's winnin's.'

'So, maybe it's not why he got shot. Maybe there was other stuff,' Ruben said. 'I think you're wanted,' he added when someone at the far end of the bar held up an empty glass.

A moment later, Ruben was thinking about Drew Desmond's widow. How long it would be before she returned to town?

6

Quinnel was astir with grim-faced people sweating in the sultry heat of the afternoon. Boardwalk loungers slumped in their deckchairs and rockers, watched the passers-by. A small group who were crossing the wheel-rutted main street, stopped quickly, moved aside as two riders galloped through.

The two men hauled in at the saloon on the far side of town. They jumped to the ground, tied their mounts to the rail. They stepped on to the boardwalk, pushed their way brusquely past a couple of pedestrians. The bigger of the two shoved the bat wings open and walked into the saloon.

'Hey, barman,' he shouted, rattling his knuckles on the bar.

The barman gave the newcomer an unresponsive look, continued to look at the quality of his glass polishing.

'You talkin' to me?' he growled.

'Do you work the night?' the big-framed man asked.

The barman put the glass down, took a closer look at the men who both showed signs of hard riding. Their shirts were damp with sweat, trail dust had set into the wrinkles of their scowling faces.

'Who wants to know?'

'Captain Morgan Lines of the Arkansas Militia. I'm looking for some information.'

'Then why not start with a more civil manner? Especially if you're wantin' somethin'?' the barman retorted. 'I'm not one o' your buck privates.'

'Don't get smart, dogboy,' the second man drawled. 'You'll end up losin' your tongue.'

Lines turned quickly. 'I'll handle this, Coop,' he said.

Ex-sergeant Cooper shrugged and moved a little to one side. He looked discomfited, leaned sullenly against the bar.

'An' in case you didn't know it, the War's been over for four months, Captain,' the barman continued. 'If you want me to help you out, lighten up an' . . . '

His voice trailed off as Lines's eyes locked with his. The big man's hand moved towards his gun-belt, and for a moment the barman thought he was going to be gunned down. His hand fell below the bar. He had to stoop slightly, searching for the scattergun that was kept on a shelf below the unbranded liquors.

Lines smiled crookedly. 'No need for that,' he warned. 'Besides, Coop here really will rip your face apart, before you get to use whatever it is you got down there.'

The other drinkers at the bar now scrambled away, backing into the tables in their haste to move from possible lines of fire.

Lines turned and faced them. 'Come on back,' he said. 'There's not going to be any gunplay. No one's going to get hurt.' He paused meaningfully. 'Not unless the barman wants otherwise.'

The barman spread his hands on top of the bar. He looked at Cooper, waiting for Lines to say more.

'A man was shot in this saloon last night,' Lines said. 'I want the full story.'

'Then go see the sheriff. He'll tell you what you need to know.'

Lines leaned forward. 'The trouble is, feller, I want you to tell me. Then I'll decide if it's what I need to know.'

'There ain't much,' the barman started. 'A feller walks in an' asks for whiskey. He wasn't quiet or loud . . . just normal like. Then this other feller comes in an' wants to shoot him in the back. The first feller who must have seen him in the mirror, turns and puts a bullet in his belly. It was all real quick. The sheriff arrived, but by then the first feller was away on his toes. My bar got smashed up a bit, but that's about it.'

'What did he look like? The first feller drinking here at the bar.'

'He was big, about your size . . . clothes looked like they were gunny sack . . . nothin' special. As I said, it was all over that quick.'

'Did he tell you his name?'

'No, of course he didn't. Why the hell would he?'

Lines looked across to his sergeant. 'Perhaps we'll visit the sheriff after all,' he said, and without another word, turned away from the bar.

As the two men pushed out through the bat wings, the barman exchanged a hostile look with Cooper.

'Don't hail from West Point, that's for sure,' he mumbled, then went about his business.

Out on the boardwalk, Cooper stared around him. 'He wasn't much help, Cap'n,' he said. 'Do you reckon he knows more?'

Lines drew a half-smoked cheroot from his top pocket. 'Hard to say. I can't think why he'd lie.'

'So what's to do now?'

'We'll pay the law a visit. Perhaps the

sheriff has got something the barman hasn't.'

The two men climbed up on their horses and rode to the jail. The years of authority in the army had left Morgan Lines with the idea that ordinary folk were at his bidding. Like most bad officers he was arrogant, and like most bullies he was sadistic. Sergeant Cooper was much the same breed, as the treatment of men under him would have testified.

Billy Reese was seated at his desk as the intruders strode into his office. He stayed silent as Lines swung the gate open and strode up to his desk. His eyes narrowed, controlling a rising surge of anger.

'The last man who came at me like that, I near shot his foot off. You're standin' right on the bullet hole,' Reese said.

Lines was cut short for a moment, then, ignoring the threat, he said, 'Are you the sheriff?'

'If I'm wearin' his badge an' sittin' in

his chair, then you can reckon on me bein' him,' Reese replied. 'Now, unless you give me a good reason for bustin' in here, I'm ready to do you serious harm,' he warned.

Lines held the law in similar indifference to that of all civilians. 'No, you're not,' he said firmly. 'We're chasing a no-account who goes by the title of Ruben Byrd. Traitor and deserter. It's getting so that we don't have the time or inclination for niceties.'

'Well, I haven't got him. Unless you think he's hidin' under one o' the bunks back there. Besides, if he's a no-account, why such a ruckus?'

'It's the army that wants him. I'm Captain Lines. This here's Sergeant Cooper. We understand you chased Byrd out of town.'

Reese walked around the desk and stood in front of Lines. He estimated that the captain and sergeant were a pair of impatient, hard-boiled soldiers. One circuit judge who regularly visited

Quinnel thought that the only differences between those who rode the owl hoot, and army officers or sheriffs of Tombstone, were buttons and badges. After the War . . . even more so.

'You ain't wearin' a uniform . . . even a goddamn badge,' Reese accused Lines.

Lines gave a short, hollow laugh. 'The Volunteers weren't much for uniforms, Sheriff. The most I had was an orange cockade.'

'They've been disbanded, goddamnit,' Reese exploded. 'You're about as much a Volunteer as my jailhouse mouser.' He thrust his chin forward, his eyes blazing angrily. 'I'll give you an' your stooge thirty seconds to clear out of my office.'

Cooper flexed his fingers eagerly. But Lines shook his head. 'I've always reckoned a man should be king of his own castle,' he said. 'Perhaps I've got us off on the wrong foot.'

'Yeah, goddamn right you have. If you'd asked proper, you could've had your information, such as it is,' Reese offered. 'You said Byrd was a traitor an' a deserter. Are you bounty hunters?'

'Does it really matter who and what we are?' Lines drawled. 'But if it makes you any happier, we lost a lot of good men at Jonesboro. For me an' Coop, it's not just the money.'

'No, it never is,' Reese grated. He couldn't see these two having friends or associates who they'd seek justice for. 'So what is it you want to know? I've already said there ain't much,' he said, pushing past Lines to regain his chair.

'Everything you've got. We've been on his tail for months,' Lines answered. 'We heard about this shooting, and the description of the feller who did it tallied with Ruben Byrd.'

Reese related much the same as the barman. He added the result of the chase and how they'd lost Byrd somewhere along Strawberry River.

Lines's face held a look of disdain as he listened. His opinion of Reese wasn't any higher than it had been. To him, any lawman who'd let a wanted man walk, ride or swim past him when he was that close to capture, was an incompetent fool.

'Where'd you bury the feller who got shot?' he demanded.

'We didn't. We've still got him. Anyone who don't die from natural causes, like gettin' shot, we have to keep a record . . . a likeness. Once a month we get a visit from a circuit photographer, but him an' his wagon ain't come through yet. You get to see the real thing.'

'So where the hell is he?'

'Out back o' the livery. He's wrapped up in three barrels o' salt from the mercantile, an' three o' charcoal from the smithy. Doc says it'll keep him fresh for a month or so.'

Lines's manner partially relaxed. He turned to Cooper. 'Sounds like we got ourselves a break at last.' He turned back to Reese. 'So we can go and see him?'

Reese shrugged. 'Can't see what

good it'll do. He sure ain't goin' to tell you anything.' He rose quickly from his chair, grabbed his hat from the peg and walked through the swing gate.

The string of stores and sheds were annexed to the side of the livery, in the lee of the taller buildings that faced the main street. When Reese lifted the latch and pulled the door open, a musky, chemical odour curled towards the three men.

Reese went inside, stepped up to a long, coffin-like box that was supported on two sawbucks. He lifted the hinged lid, standing aside to hold it open. Lines brushed aside a heap of charcoal, lifted one end of a blanket that was stiff, caked with salt. He leaned forward, cursing quietly when he saw the white, waxen features beneath.

'I don't remember where or when, but I've seen this man before,' he said.

Cooper moved close to take a look. 'Yeah, that's him. McSwane. Weren't exactly keen on volunteerin', I recall. Must've been even less so on gettin' sold out. There must've been a few more who wanted to get their hands on Byrd,' he said. 'But he wouldn't have known him, would he?' he added after a moment's thought.

Lines stared at the dead face again. 'He could have. When we went back to Fort Clinton, most of the company had a good look at him.'

'Do you figure McSwane was huntin' him?'

'From what you've just said, I wouldn't have thought so,' Reese cut in. 'Besides, from what Len tells me, he was hangin' about town before Byrd rode in. Byrd was just ridin' through.'

'Who's Len?'

'Barman.'

Lines dropped the blanket back and turned to the door.

Cooper jerked his thumb in the direction of McSwane's body. 'One o' them Jonesboro field surgeons would've got him fixed up an' back into battle,' he sniped.

Lines ignored him. 'What's the next

town, heading west?' he asked, as Reese closed the shed door. 'Some place with more'n a well and a bench.'

'Vinegar Wells. It's a good two days' ride from here, though. You reckon he's headed that way?'

'He's been headed west so far. It's about all we've got to go on.'

As they walked back towards the jail, Lines was lost in thought. 'It could have been chance that McSwane stumbled on Byrd,' he said after a few minutes. 'But why would he want to backshoot him? All he had to do was call in the law to collect $1,000. It doesn't make sense.'

Reese nodded as though he was thinking, in agreement.

'You know what, Sheriff?' Lines continued. 'We caught Byrd, but I'm thinking McSwane was the other one . . . the second one. They arranged to meet here, but McSwane went for the double-cross. He probably couldn't bear living with the worry of knowing what he did. It made him vulnerable.'

Reese rubbed his hand across his chin. 'Hmm, that makes more sense.'

'Coop, get the horses,' Lines ordered. 'We're riding for Vinegar Wells.'

'Sure, Cap'n,' Cooper replied, throwing a token salute.

Lines returned to Reese and held out his hand 'Like I said, Sheriff, some of those men who were cut down down at Jonesboro were friends.'

Sheriff Reese eyed the hand for the shortest moment, then offered Lines an icy stare.

'Not of yours, though,' he muttered and strode back towards his office.

7

Ruben Byrd was perched on the rocks at a bend in the trail two miles outside of Vinegar Wells. He felt it would be more prudent for him to keep away from town until he saw Drew Desmond's widow and spoke with her. With a hanged murderer removed from the equation, his predicament was narrowed down to Desmond and Fergus Stearne. He mulled over Harry the barman's disclosure that Stearne was an army man. If Stearne had been in the Volunteers, then he knew more about Ruben than he was letting on. *Yeah, good act*, Ruben thought. *The son-of-a-bitch knows and he's keeping quiet.*

Deciding to meet the weekly stage-coach from Black Rock and Beaver Lakes, he took his time riding back to town. The scheduled noon arrival was more than two hours overdue, but he stopped for another few minutes beside the long curling bend in the river. It was where the trail ran close to the rail track, and he let the roan snatch at wayside grass.

At the depot, he stood at the end of the passenger platform, watching patiently as Mrs Desmond arranged for her trunk to be taken out to her house. There was much vigorous talk between the driver and the stage representative, but, interesting though it might be, it wasn't what Ruben had come for.

'Mrs Desmond, my name's Ruben Byrd,' he introduced himself. 'There's something we need to discuss. Something *I* need to discuss, anyway. I've been waiting a while,' he added with an easy smile.

'Yes, we're late. The coach was attacked by a group of masked men outside of Black Rock. At the Lakes they brought a body in, and we had to wait for a new driver. It was all very discomforting. You don't want to

110

discuss that, do you?'

'No, no. Would it be more convenient later on this evening?'

'Is it something to do with Drew?' she replied. Then, frowning slightly, she gave him a closer look. 'You're not a lawman, are you?'

The question surprised Ruben. 'No, not any kind,' he said. 'But it is your husband I wanted to talk about.'

For a moment, Mrs Desmond looked as though she was going to change her mind. Instead, she nodded acceptance. 'My house is white-painted brick. As such you can't miss it. It's just beyond the end of Main, by the last tree on the left. If it's important, come by in an hour.'

'Thanks. I'll see you then.' Ruben looked up as Mrs Desmond walked out, and George Jasper touched his Stetson walking in.

'Howdy, Sheriff. Strange why bad news should travel faster than good,' he said.

Jasper gave Ruben a short, quizzical

look. 'I usually meet the stage at this time. Drivers see an' hear things other folk sometimes don't bother with. You know . . . the detail.'

'Yeah. It sounds as if this one might have something for you. Mrs Desmond looks like a nice lady.'

'She is. As far as her husband's concerned, there's no accountin' for taste.'

'Yeah. I told her I wanted to see her about her husband. From what I've overheard, you'll be having other stuff to work on for a while. So I hope that's OK.'

Jasper nodded positively. 'Just make sure it is.'

Along the street, and at the rear of the Applejack Room, a man reined in his horse. He climbed arduously from the saddle, his legs buckling as he made it to the ground. He lurched to the staircase, took a searching look around him before dragging himself up to the second-storey landing.

★ ★ ★

112

Mrs Desmond was waiting on the front porch of her house when Ruben rode up. She straightened up from her chair, and walked to the low balustrade, watched as he dismounted and tied his horse to the rail.

'There's coffee inside,' she said, turning and opening the screen door. 'Have you any idea what the sheriff's going to do about the hold-up?'

'I don't see what he can do. Unless the driver's got something for him to go on, he'll have to wait for more news. But I expect he'll already be chewing on the meat of it. George started on being a lawman from the age of four.'

She gave a look of mild surprise. 'You know George Jasper . . . the sheriff?'

'Yeah, I know him. We grew up together. Not seen him for quite a while, though.'

She took Ruben's words in. Showing him into the parlour, she told him to make himself comfortable while she went to fetch the coffee.

Ruben looked around him. The

touch of a female hand was clear to see and not displeasing. The windows were framed by lacy curtains and the mantelshelf was covered with a runner and pictures of what Ruben supposed were Mrs Desmond and her family. He placed his hat on a round-topped table, noted the antimacassars draped over the backs of the chairs. He sat by the window, self-consciously felt the hair at the back of his head, looked at his boots on the bright red Ganado rug. Rising from the floor was a tall, Chinese patterned vase that contained a spray of dry grasses. Ruben smiled at being surrounded by so much refinement. *Don't suppose I'm adding much*, he thought wryly.

He eased back in the chair, felt mechanically for where he usually kept his chaw tobacco. He was wiping his mouth with the back of his hand in anticipation, when Mrs Desmond returned.

When she'd poured the coffee, Mrs Desmond placed an occasional table between them and sat opposite. 'Sugar?' she asked.

Ruben gave an enthusiastic nod. 'It's been a long time since I sat like this in a real house,' he said.

'You've no home?'

'No ma'am, no home. And some of the places I've ate and slept in can hardly be called places. I've been on the move, you see.' Ruben placed the cup on the table, felt his empty pocket again.

Mrs Desmond went to the end of the mantelshelf and picked up a decorated wooden box. 'Help yourself to one of these,' she said. 'It's a shame letting them go to waste. They're Havana, I believe.'

Ruben took one of the cigars held it to his nose and sniffed favourably.

'I'm guessing it's a long time since you've smoked one of those,' she smiled.

'A long time never.'

'Did you say it was my husband you wanted to talk about?' Mrs Desmond asked.

'Yes, ma'am.'

'Well, while you're sitting in my home, smoking his cigars, I think you should call me Annie. And please don't concern yourself with what's proper and what isn't. We were never close enough for me to grieve. As for anyone else . . . who cares.'

Ruben smiled. 'Suits me. I'll be Ruben.'

'Fine. Now tell me what brings you here, Ruben.' Annie Desmond leaned back in her chair. She lifted her cup, and sipped slowly.

'It's a long story and not a particularly agreeable one,' Ruben started. 'Can I start by asking if your husband was ever in the army?'

'Yes, he was,' Annie replied, her voice showing no particular shade. 'Why?'

Ruben looked towards the pictures on the mantelshelf, noticed there was one of a wedding scene. He lit the cigar, took a couple of satisfying puffs as he thought. Annie stayed quiet as he told her his story, why he was in Vinegar Wells.

'So there you have it, Annie. It's either your husband or Fergus Stearne that I'm looking for. It's also the reason I've no home to go to.'

It was Ruben's last remark that kept Annie quiet. She stared at the grounds in the cup, then at the cigar between Ruben's fingers. Her face had grown pale as her mind worked to take in and retain all that he'd told her.

'I expect George Jasper believes you?' she said eventually.

'I think . . . hope he does. Whether the sheriff of Vinegar Wells does, is a different matter, if you get my meaning.'

'Yes, I understand, Ruben.'

'At least he's given me some time. That's why I had to talk to you. Whatever the outcome, it's important you believe me, Annie.'

'Why? *I'm* not going to hang you.'

Ruben smiled bleakly. 'No, I know.' He paused and looked directly at her. 'If your husband was the one who turned traitor, I'll be asking you to betray him. You're still his widow.'

It was Annie's turn to smile. 'Listen Ruben, Drew's dead and can't be hurt. I was married to him long enough to not worry about sullying his name . . . our name. And I won't be carrying *that* forever. I often wonder what it was that induced me to marry him in the first place. Besides, if he was the one who turned traitor, I'll hardly be betraying him. If the truth's going to come out, what am I supposed to do?'

Ruben smoked the cigar. Even though the circumstances were sensitive, he felt more relaxed, mellower in the company of Annie Desmond. He reflected that she was the type of woman he could possibly settle down with. There was a fondness for her already growing inside him.

'We were married in Little Rock . . . booked into a nice hotel,' Annie went on. 'It was early evening. He said he was going out, that he'd be back in a while. I was certain it was going to be a surprise, you know, flowers or some-thing.' Annie took a deep breath, gathering her emotions. 'It was a surprise all right. He came in after midnight, drunk as a skunk. I'd spent hours making myself look nice for him, arranging the room.'

Ruben squirmed uneasily in his chair. He wanted to say, 'minutes, surely', but didn't.

Annie smiled unhappily as she called the scene to mind. 'It was my wedding night, for heaven's sake, and he collapsed on to the bed . . . just passed out. How he even got back, I don't know.' She looked at Ruben, paused as her eyes misted with the memory. 'And that was the first of every night from then on. The same story. How could it be, Ruben? Not just married to an unlucky gambler, but a drunkard.'

'And blind.'

'Blind?'

'He had *you*. He didn't see it.'

'I think we were both guilty of that. I had a small amount of money saved.

He started going through that when he lost what *he* had. I couldn't take it any more . . . told him that unless he stopped, I'd leave him. So we left Little Rock for a new start.'

'Why here?'

'I heard about the railroad, that it was a decent town and on the up. Somewhere with a future. Huh. For others, I guess,' she continued, looking up at the pictures on the mantelshelf. 'I used most of what I had to bring us here. I thought it was for the best . . . the right thing. But I was wrong. Vinegar Wells was just the top of another slippery slope.'

Ruben shook his head. It was beyond his comprehension how any man could have disregarded Annie for the sake of a card game or a bottle.

Annie's anxiety increased as she guessed Ruben's thoughts. She went on again, quickly. 'We took an upstairs room at the Applejack. There wasn't much else, but it didn't help, with tables actually at arm's length. But if

Little Rock was the frying pan, this place was the fire. He started losing from the first deal.'

'But that changed, didn't it?' Ruben offered.

'Yes. One night he came home with money. More than we'd seen in a long time. Wads of it, all big bills. 'Bad times are behind us, Annie. From now on it's purple an' fine linen,'' he said. And he was right, Ruben. We were able to buy this house and furnish it. I asked him what had happened, but he'd just smile and tap the side of his nose. I thought it was what every delusional gambler dreams of . . . getting touched by a guardian angel's lucky stick.'

'Did you ask him about it . . . the money?'

'Yes. He said it didn't have anything to do with luck, anymore — that Fergus Stearne couldn't afford to let him lose. I thought perhaps he was being paid as the Applejack's advertisement for gambling . . . to draw in the punters. The bunko steerer.'

'But it wasn't?'

'No, of course not. Nothing as honest as that.'

'So what did you think?'

'Eventually, that he was paying Drew to keep quiet. Drew must have had something on him from a time I knew nothing of.'

'He must have dropped a hint sometime. When he'd got himself roostered?'

Annie shook her head. 'I know they were both in the Volunteer Militia, that's all.'

'Oh, that's not all, Annie. But let's not get ahead of ourselves. Right this moment I'm likely to put two and two together and get ten,' Ruben said eagerly, trying to control the urge to yell of a success. 'You're confirming a festering thought. It's the lead I wanted . . . your husband knowing something about Stearne. Or that they were — '

'Involved in something else?' Annie interrupted. 'That Drew might have been shot because of it . . . whatever it was?'

'Two and two's making more than ten now, Annie.' Ruben had pushed himself up from the chair, his mind running on.

Annie realized it and got up to face him. 'What are you thinking?'

'I'm wondering why you didn't tell all this to the sheriff . . . George,' Ruben said.

'I don't know. He didn't ask me too many questions, and it didn't seem important at the time. I'm only now putting any meaning together. I had no reason before.'

'No reason?'

'Not about any connivance between them, no. Besides — and I'm not proud of it — having the house and money took the edge off all the misery. That's awful sounding, but it's not as though he was knocking me about.'

'I understand. I reckon that's enough for now,' Ruben decided. He pushed the cigar into the side of his mouth, picked up his hat, and walked towards the door. 'I'll pay George a visit . . . come back later and let you know what's to be.'

Annie smiled. 'We'll have supper. I'm sure I can provide something more substantial than coffee and cigars.' Then she stepped up and placed a hand on his arm.

Ruben could see loneliness in her eyes and he shuffled his feet uncomfortably, trying to suppress the notion there was something between them.

'It's the timing, Ruben,' she said. 'I need a friend more than I thought. I think we both do.'

Ruben returned her smile. 'Yeah. We've sure had our lives messed about.' He looked at her for a moment, then closed the door quietly behind him and headed for the jailhouse.

8

Fergus Stearne was sitting in his upstairs study at the Applejack Room. He was resting easy in a large, leather chair, cleaning his fingernails with the tip of a Barlow knife. He'd been aware of the commotion in the street when the stage had arrived, knew it was for more than being a few hours late. Harry the barman had brought him news of the hold-up, and now his manner was one of fretful thought.

He was considering the timing, how much of it had passed, when the door to his office burst open. A man wearing range clothes, and with one hand holding his stomach, staggered into the room.

Stearne immediately jumped to his feet. 'Maggie, goddamn it,' he rasped, spiking the open bladed knife into his desk top. 'What the hell's going on? I told you not to come back here, no matter what.'

'It was the Clampetts, boss. They lit out on me, an' I got hit. I think I'm hurt bad,' the man named Maggie gasped.

'Did anyone see you come up here?'

'No, no one. Where was I supposed to go for chris'sakes? I've got a bullet in me.'

Stearne grimaced and cursed. He walked around the desk and stood close to Maggie, drew aside a piece of sodden shirt for a look at the wound.

'You've probably had worse things in your pouch,' he said. 'You won't be dying just yet.' He poured a glass of whiskey from his decanter, offered it to the wounded man.

Maggie swallowed hard, wiped his hand at the dribble on his chin and gave the glass back.

'What happened out there? What went wrong?' Stearne demanded.

Maggie grunted. His lean, lined face was twisted in pain as he breathed, his

126

grimy, blood-stained fingers clutching together at his middle.

'We were unlucky. Hell, I don't know,' he groaned, looking desperately at Stearne.

'Why the hell did you run? There was three of you, goddamnit.'

'An' the company had a full team out there. Black Rock's their new swing station. They rode with a shotgun messenger as well. We got their second driver . . . that was all. We were outnumbered.'

'Did they recognize you? Any of you?'

'No, we were covered up enough . . . didn't get too close. I hurt real bad, boss.'

'Yeah, you shouldn't have had the whiskey. Are you sure no one's seen you coming into town?'

'I already said,' Maggie gasped. He felt his strength ebbing, saw the cool indifference of Stearne. He cursed and ground his teeth when he realized there was nothing being done to help him. He drew his Colt, brought the barrel high up into Stearne's chest.

'What the hell are you doing?' Stearne's coldness suddenly became anxiety.

'I know too much ... suddenly become a problem for you,' Maggie charged. 'You're figurin' on havin' me die right here.'

'Don't be a fool,' Stearne protested. 'The pain and the whiskey's addled your brain. Put your goddamn pistol away.'

'Just take me somewhere to get taken care of.'

Stearne shrugged. 'Right away, if that's what you want,' he said.

He walked to his hat and coat stand, was doing some hurried thinking when a wracking cough tore through Maggie's body. He turned to see the man's arm drooping, the pistol close to falling from his rigid fingers.

'For all the good it'll do,' he muttered, reaching for the hideout gun that was in its shoulder holster hanging beneath his Stetson. With his hat in his left hand covering his right, he stepped quickly up to Maggie. Without moving his hat aside, he pushed the small gun up against the distraught man's fingers.

'Help me, boss,' Maggie grated.

'Like a horse for the canner,' Stearne responded quietly and pulled the trigger.

The sound of the single shot was muffled, didn't sound mortal. But Maggie gasped, then stiffened under the impact of the close-range bullet. As he buckled, Stearne took a step back, watched as Maggie tried in vain to raise his pistol. Then the man closed his eyes and fell dead.

Stearne took a further step back. 'Sorry, friend, you really shouldn't have come here.'

He folded his damaged Stetson around his gun, and placed them together in a side drawer of his desk. Then he wiped the sweat from his forehead, straightened his coat and poured himself a whiskey. He had to get rid of Maggie's body. He looked around him, thought away from the centre of the room would be OK until full dark. Then he noticed the Turkoman rug, staining with Maggie's blood.

'Goddamn new carpet as well as a hat,' he sighed.

Taking a key from his waistcoat, he stepped out on to the landing. He quietly shut and locked the door, tested its closure and headed for the staircase.

* * *

Lines and Cooper reined in outside the Vinegar Wells jail. Lines raised himself in the stirrups and looked along the main street. A slight, satisfied smile crossed his face and he nodded to the former sergeant. 'Not a bad looking town, Coop. Better than most we've been through lately.'

'That ain't sayin' much,' Cooper drawled. 'Let's hope Byrd's here. I'm sick to the back teeth o' chasin' him.'

Lines scowled. 'Trouble with you, Coop, you want your money too easy. I'll chase him right across Arkansas and swim the Mississippi for a thousand dollars. So why don't you shut your whining and we'll go see what this lawman has to say.'

The two men hitched their lathered mounts to the rail and stepped to the boardwalk. Lines stopped at the door and turned to Cooper.

'Remember, some of these law officers are very cautious . . . proddy, too,' he warned. 'Let's go in easy.'

George Jasper was sitting at his desk, his head down, reading through papers. He was bothered about the stage hold-up outside Black Rock. He had no evidence and very little information to go on, but doubted anyone in Vinegar Wells would be involved in the attempted theft of a silver bullion shipment. He looked up when Lines and Cooper entered the office.

'Somethin' I can do for you, gents?'

he asked casually. He recognized them as strangers, was hoping there might be something different he could put his mind to.

'Maybe,' Lines answered. 'We're looking for information. I know you lawmen like a civil exchange, so I'm asking real polite.'

'I really wouldn't expect it any other way. An' that's me bein' polite,' Jasper said, waving them over to his desk. 'Information about what?'

'We're searching for a man named Byrd . . . Ruben Byrd. We reckon he's headed this way.'

Jasper's eyes narrowed. He leaned back in his swivel chair and picked up his pipe, turned the bowl meditatively in his fingers.

Lines shifted irritably. 'Looks like you're making some thinking time,' he said.

'I'm thinkin' all right. I'm thinkin' that if he is headed this way, he can't have got here yet. You two got names?'

'Arkansas towns are right full o'

smart-alecky sheriffs, Cap'n,' Cooper sneered.

Jasper remained very still, his eyes swivelling to Cooper. 'You got a mount outside?' he asked calmly.

'Yeah, what of it?'

'Just wondered.' Jasper turned to Lines, aimed the stem of his pipe at him. 'Are you the wirepuller o' this little outfit?'

'I'm Captain Morgan Lines, and he's Sergeant Cooper,' the ex-officer said severely. 'And if you've read all the circuit papers and dodgers carefully, you'll know what we're after Byrd for.'

Jasper gave a spare smile. 'I know damn well who Byrd is, Captain Lines. An' I also know what he's wanted for. So what are you a captain of?'

'Volunteers. The Volunteer Militia.'

Jasper puffed his cheeks unenthusiastically. 'We had a war that lasted four goddamn years, an' for some o' you, it's just not enough,' he said. 'As far as I'm concerned, you're Lines an' he's Cooper. So don't try an' intimidate or

133

impress me with bogus titles.'

Lines's face coloured, and an eyelid flickered with anger. 'I'm not. I want Byrd,' he said.

'What you goin' to do when . . . *if* you find him? Apart from collect the reward money, that is?'

Cooper took a step closer to his captain. 'You got a smart mouth for a sheriff, an' no respect for army rank,' he snarled at Jasper.

'What I have got, is eyes an' ears workin' for me. Anythin' bad happens in this office, there's no way you're goin' to make it on to that horse outside.' Jasper's voice was controlled, quietly menacing. 'In fact, much more from you, an' I'll forget that politeness I mentioned. Now, tell me about this Byrd feller.'

'He ratted on the company . . . sold them out,' Lines replied. 'I lost a lot of men, as did Sergeant Cooper. The money's just a veneer.'

Jasper nodded. 'If what you say's true, I guess you would have a personal interest,' he conceded. 'But bad things happen in war . . . very bad things. So I reckon it is the $1,000 that's got you an' your sergeant galloping across Arkansas. It's nothin' to do with avengin' fellow soldiers. You're usin' a captain's commission when an' where you can, to chase down that reward.'

'And your job's to uphold the law,' Lines barked. 'We haven't ridden all this way to get obstructed by a goddamn janitor man.'

Jasper grinned. 'I reckon you have,' he replied derisively. 'An' don't tell me my job.' He turned to Cooper who had started to move around the desk. 'Get back where I can see you. I don't much like snakes slidin' around behind me.'

Cooper muttered a curse, but returned to stand beside Lines.

Jasper then got to his feet and faced the two men. 'Byrd is in town. An' he's my prisoner. Chew on that for a moment.'

There was stunned silence as Jasper's

disclosure sunk in. Cooper continued his cursing.

'He's here? You've got him locked up?' Lines asked, his disappointment palpable.

'Nope. But I'm keepin' him under wraps . . . a sort o' curfew. You've probably heard of it as bail.'

'Bail? You've got the goddamn traitor out on bail?' Lines snapped. 'What the hell sort of lawman are you?'

'A just one. Byrd says he's come here to prove he's innocent, so I've given him forty-eight hours to do just that. If he doesn't, I'll lock him up an' send for the army. The real, existent army.'

Lines's face suddenly broke into a cunning smile, and Jasper guessed the thinking behind it. He also wished he knew where Ruben Byrd was and what he was doing.

'If I was you, I'd forget that thought,' he said quietly.

'What's he talkin' about, Cap'n? What are you thinkin'?' Cooper asked.

'If Byrd is around, he's thinkin' he'll

take him, probably put a bullet in him,' Jasper answered. 'Money doesn't usually make a distinction between dead an' alive. That's right, eh, Lines?'

'Yeah, you know it,' Lines said. 'You let him out, and now he's fair game. The consequences are all down to you, Sheriff.'

'Listen to me. He's my prisoner. Kill him an' you'll hang for murder. Try an' ride out o' town with him, an' you'll hang for kidnappin'. An' I'll tell you another thing. You've got two days to clear town. It's what I gave Byrd.'

Lines's face clouded and his voice dropped. 'We've done nothing wrong. There's no wanted posters on us. There's nothing you can do.'

'That's where you're wrong,' Jasper said. 'As you say, I'm the law in this town, an' I'm gettin' madder by the minute. I don't want you in Vinegar Wells. *Comprendez?*'

Lines stood his ground for a minute while he fumed, hardly suppressed anger crawling through his body.

'Let me show you somethin' more convincin',' Jasper continued. Leaning towards his desk, he opened a side drawer and calmly took out a big Walker Colt. 'I can see you come from gummy old stock, Mr Captain. So let me try an' grease things up a bit,' he grated. 'If you don't clear my office now, I'll put one .44 bullet in you, an' another in your dog robber friend here. Later, I'll drag your bodies to the pens out back o' the nearest chop suey joint an' feed you to the pigs. By first light tomorrow, there'll be nary a boot heel left. You won't even be a goddamn memory.'

Cooper gave a short, dull snort of a laugh. 'You reckon he can do that, Cap'n?' he asked slowly.

'Yeah, I reckon, Coop. He is mad enough. And in this town, he does whatever he wants, irrespective of the law he espouses, or of being just.'

The sheriff actioned the big Colt's hammer. 'If you were regular army it would be different. But you're not.

You're nothin' more'n goddamn bounty hunters. Get out,' he rasped, with a gesture.

Jasper stood in the thunderous silence as the two men mounted their horses, smiled icily as they wheeled away and rode off down the main street. He didn't think he'd won, but was fairly certain their brazenness had been tempered. Any man who used a badge of office to hide behind, couldn't be all that dangerous. *Gimme a cannon anytime*, he thought, and smiled again. He tried to dismiss them from his mind in favour of the stage hold-up. Ten minutes later he was still pacing his office, about to give up and begin his walk around town when the door opened once again. This time Ruben Byrd walked in.

Jasper stepped around his desk and pushed the drawer shut. 'Where the hell've you been?' he demanded.

'And good evening to you, George,' Ruben responded. 'I've been getting myself the break I need. But I think I

139

need you to fill in a few gaps.'

Jasper nodded. 'You wouldn't think it was much of a break if you'd been here ten minutes ago.'

'Why, what's happened?'

'Two ex-army just rode in, an' they're not goin' to ride out, until they've nailed your hide.'

'Hell,' Ruben swore. 'Ex-army, you say?'

'Yeah, ex-Volunteer men. But now they're bounty hunters, an' a more disagreeable pair I haven't mixed with since I don't know when.'

Ruben swore again and slumped into one of Jasper's visitor's chairs. 'Apart from nailing my hide, what did they say they wanted? You're not thinking of handing me over, are you?' he said.

'You think I'd do that, Rube?'

Ruben shook his head. 'No. But I bet a lot of men have been undone for the want of it.' A sheepish smile spread over his face as he saw Jasper consider what he'd said. Then he calmed as he saw that it wasn't the personal stuff that was concerning his friend, the sheriff. 'What's got you worried?' he asked.

'A pair o' ill-natured turkey cocks. One named Lines, the other one Cooper. They're still using their army rank.'

'Lines?' Ruben mused.

'Yeah. Captain,' he reckons.

'I can't put a face to it. There was a captain in the Volunteers, I know that.'

Jasper picked up his pipe again, made the same deliberation of twisting it around in his fingers before he spoke. He knew that what he was going to say would antagonize Ruben, but he believed it to be the only way. 'Rube, I'm goin' to lock you up,' he drawled calmly.

'Huh. I thought I was the one having daft thoughts,' Ruben countered.

'I'm serious, Rube. Just think, would you trust a lawman who let a renegade run free . . . a fugitive from the law, without due consideration? Do you think a sheriff should make legal dispensation for an old friend?' Jasper held up his hand to stop Ruben answering back. 'No need to answer, Rube. You're thinkin' the answer's yes. An' you're right, god-damnit,' he continued.

'Would that be the same sheriff who gave his old friend two days to get sorted?'

'Hell, Ruben, you'd never live it out. Not now. Things have changed,' Jasper said. 'This Morgan Lines is a field o' blood merchant, if ever there's been one. An' Cooper's a dangerous lap dog, who obviously does his bidding. Until I can get them both away from town, I figure the only safe place for you is behind bars.'

'Making me a sitting duck, George, an' you know it. A piece of live bait. Are you going to stay here guarding me day and night? Thanks, but no thanks, Sheriff. I'd rather take my chances hiding out in the river with the cottonmouths.'

Jasper wiped a hand across his forehead and cursed quietly. In a way

Ruben was right. He couldn't watch the jail twenty-four hours a day, and if he let him free, there was a certainty there'd be a shooting. Jasper also knew that running Lines and Cooper out of town would serve little purpose. His jurisdiction only stretched to the county line, and the nearest boundary was only four miles to the south. There was nothing to stop the two men from camping beyond the line, and slipping back whenever they wanted.

There was also the town's present concern about the stage being held up, not to mention the killing of Drew Desmond. As he contemplated the problems, he watched Ruben take a cigar stub from his pocket and set it between his lips, one side of his mouth.

'So, what did you come to see me about anyway?' he asked finally. 'You said, you've got a break . . . need me for somethin'.'

'Yeah, that's right, George. That, and why it wouldn't be a great idea to lock me up right now. I had that talk with

Mrs Desmond, and she's come up with some real fascinating stuff.' Ruben then told Jasper what Annie Desmond had held back previously . . . and why.

Jasper gave a meaningful groan when Ruben mentioned the possibility of Desmond blackmailing Fergus Stearne.

'Damn me for a slowpoke, Rube. The lady's not the only one who can forget or overlook things,' he said. 'Of course, it make sense now.'

'What does?'

'The time I was in the saloon. Stearne an' Desmond were at one of the tables. Whatever it was, I've never seen Stearne so heated. His face was the colour of one of his plush seats. If he'd had a gun in his hand, he'd have used it, that's for sure. It seemed natural for me to ask if everythin' was OK, but they both said it was nothin'. I'd dread to think what would've happened if it had been *something*. Anyways, I accepted it an' left shortly after. Hell, Rube, it wasn't long after that, that Desmond started on his lucky streak. If only I'd thought it out . . . '

Ruben shook his head. 'You couldn't. You didn't know then, what you know now,' he said. '*But*, if Desmond did know of Stearne's secret, perhaps they were at odds over the size of payment . . . the blood money. From talking with Desmond's wife, it must have been a considerable sum, *and* regular.'

'It sure adds up,' Jasper said. An expressive smile broke across his face. 'If any o' that's true, you've got to hand it to Stearne. As a killer, he's covered himself pretty good.'

'Me and Annie Desmond were trying not to make two an' two add up to more than four,' Ruben answered. 'If it is Stearne I'm after, *nothing*'s going to help him now. *Nothing*.'

'He's the one we're *both* after, Rube. Solvin' a town shootin's down to me. Like I said before, Desmond was some sort o' cuss . . . not much liked. But no one seemed to have a reason to plug him. Now we know different, or certainly think it.'

Ruben took the cigar from his mouth, studied it, put it in a tin on Jasper's desk. 'I think I'll pay Fergus Stearne a visit. Nothing rash, George. Like a fox flushin' out a bobwhite.'

'I won't stop you, Rube . . . not now. But be real wary. If it's true . . . if he even suspects you're on to him, you're dead meat. He'll have to eliminate you. The thought of bein' exposed must be like livin' with a cancer. An' don't forget Lines an' Cooper. They won't have given up.'

'Have they been up to Stearne's place yet?'

'Didn't sound like it. But when they left here, they looked as though they needed more'n sarsaparilla. Hah. The good Sergeant Cooper would've chewed the top off every goddamn bottle in town.'

Ruben shrugged resignedly and pulled on his hat. 'I hope it is Stearne,' he said. 'It's got to be settled. I don't want to move on, George.' Then he nodded and walked to the door.

Pensively, Jasper went back to his chair. He too now had something to consider . . . maybe the break he needed. He had excluded all town personages from his suspicions when considering the hold-up outside Black Rock. But now, with squeaky clean Fergus Stearne getting himself dirtied, it was different. There was no doubt about Stearne knowing about the cash money shipment, and with the comings and goings of his associates, he could easily have finagled the robbery.

Jasper leaned back, closed his eyes for a moment. Omitting the regular drinkers, and gamblers, he ran through what he knew of the more likely visitors to the Applejack Room. Of those he could recall, he placed them as decent, law-abiding local townsfolk. But he knew there must be something . . . someone he'd missed.

'Going to need a drink,' he muttered.

9

Ruben tied his roan to the rail outside the Applejack Room. He crossed the boardwalk and peered in from one side of the heavy, ornate swing doors. At the far end of the saloon, he saw that Fergus Stearne was seated at his usual table, riffling a pack of playing cards. Hitching his belt, he strode to the bar, asked Harry the barman for the bottle of Old Crow and two glasses, then walked on to Stearne's table.

Stearne looked up as Ruben approached. 'Good evening. Have you come to see me about that work I mentioned, or to drink that?' he asked, amiably.

'The latter,' Ruben returned. 'Work's the curse of the drinking man,' he offered with a smile.

Stearne held his hand out to a chair. 'Then take a pew.'

Ruben sat down and poured them each a generous measure.

'The town's sure giving you a reception,' Stearne said. 'The thrill of a stage hold-up and you've hardly made a footfall.'

'Even more thrilling if you'd been travelling that route,' Ruben replied, immediately impressed with Stearne's coolness and easy manner to allay suspicion. *The hallmark of a decent poker player*, he thought. 'Still, it's an ill wind that blows *nobody* any good,' he added. 'If the stage hadn't have been late, I probably wouldn't have met who I did.'

'Who was that, might I ask?'

'Mrs Desmond. A real nice lady. But you know her, of course?'

Stearne's easy smile slipped a fraction. 'The widow Desmond? Of course, I know her. And I can understand the attraction. But I wouldn't go too fast. There could be someone else tipping their hat in that direction.'

'I'd be surprised if there wasn't,'

Ruben agreed. 'But all's fair in love and war, they say.'

'Them that say such things are usually on the winning side.'

Ruben gave a non-committed shrug and swallowed half the bourbon in his glass.

'You and I seem to have hit it off well enough,' Stearne continued. 'We wouldn't want anything to sour that. Most folk need a supporter in a town like Vinegar Wells, if you understand what I'm saying.'

'I think I get your drift. But the country's freer now than it's ever been, Mr Stearne. I guess Annie can make up her own mind,' Ruben drawled.

'Annie?' Stearne's voice suddenly hardened, his eyebrows lifting with clear irritation. 'You've certainly come a long way on such a short acquaintance with the lady.'

'I'm sorry. I seem to have inadvertently touched a raw nerve.'

'I somehow doubt there's anything inadvertent about it, Mr Byrd. But yes,

I reckon you have.'

'She told me her husband used to play cards here,' Ruben said, feigning an unawareness of Stearne's special anger. 'You and him were old army buddies, weren't you?'

Ruben watched the saloon owner's expression change. Momentarily, the man's eyes narrowed and a trace of a scowl moved his lips.

'I can imagine you'd feel obligated to look after her, if that's what this is about,' Ruben went on, intentionally running off course. 'She did tell me how much you helped her husband create a way for them to get set up financially. He was shot out back of here, wasn't he?'

Stearne was in full control of himself now. He looked at Ruben shrewdly, weighing him up as more than a rival for Annie Desmond's attention. 'Does it matter if it's more than an obligation on my part?' he asked. 'Put another way, how interested are you?'

'Must confess, I'm finding myself a

tad smitten,' Ruben said, smiling ingenuously. 'So, you being a friend an' all, I thought you'd be wanting to get your hands on the low-life who carried out the shooting. It must have been doubly bad to lose an old comrade.'

Ruben was thinking that if he'd been Stearne, by now he'd be getting really irritated. But his response was believably sincere, and Stearne was taken in, assuming that Ruben was just being inquisitive, naturally concerned.

Stearne gave a lean smile and leaned forward understandingly. 'It was. And I figured I could help Annie. Desmond was more than a regular customer. In a way, I blame myself for the shooting.'

Ruben nodded. *Yeah, you would*, he thought, staring hard at Stearne.

'Ol' Drew was reeling the night it happened,' Stearne continued. 'It could easily have been another drunk who rolled him. I should have seen he got home.'

'Hmm, maybe. It was right back of here, wasn't it?' Ruben reiterated.

Stearne nodded. 'Yeah, not long after he left the table. It must have been someone waiting for him. When his body was found he'd been cleaned out.'

Ruben poured another couple of shots. 'Must have been hard on both of you in your own ways,' he said. 'You and Desmond went through the war together, virtually unscathed. Then he gets bumped off in Piss Alley by a sneak thief. By the way, what company of the Volunteers did you say you were in?'

Ruben's question was almost a casual aside, but the effect on Stearne was astonishing. He gripped the glass of bourbon, his eyes suddenly burned.

'I didn't say,' he responded sharply, open hostility not far away. 'No reason to. The War's over, and there's much to try and forget.' He gulped down his liquor, banged the glass back on the table. 'What's done's done.'

Ruben nodded. To him, Stearne's wanting to forget and move on, was a euphemism for something to hide . . . plenty to hide. He looked around at the big clock with an elaborately painted dial. 'Assuming that grand timepiece is correct, I'd best be making a move,' he said. 'Annie's invited me for supper tonight. Least I can do is have a wash an' brush-up.'

As Ruben got to his feet, Stearne raised his eyes. 'That *someone* I mentioned who might have an interest in her direction? It was me,' he said severely. 'I don't like people treading on my toes, Byrd. So step real careful. And leave the bottle here. I've just decided the drinks are on you.'

It wasn't so much that Ruben Byrd was seeing Annie Desmond that worried Stearne. It was more the other stuff. It sounded like the man had information on him. Stearne cursed, poured himself a brimming measure of Old Crow.

* * *

Half an hour later, Stearne was still drinking sullenly. Not only did he have

154

the body of Maggie to move, but Ruben Byrd appeared to be getting his nose into things that he didn't want him to. He didn't know how or when exactly, but it looked like now was maybe when the piper got paid. He cursed long and hard.

As he stoppered the remains of the bourbon, the doors along to his left opened and two newcomers pushed in. He watched Lines and Cooper walk to the bar and order their drinks. *They've not come to play a few hands of Slippery Sam*, he thought anxiously.

When Harry the barman handed over the bottle of whiskey, Lines held his arm for a moment. 'We're looking for a feller named Byrd. Do you know of him . . . seen him in here maybe?'

Harry eyed both men. 'Who you askin' as?'

'Friends of his,' Lines answered.

'This ain't a lost an' found office, mister, but I happen to know he was drinkin' with the boss not so long ago. Maybe he can help you.' Harry nodded in the direction of Stearne.

Lines placed some coins on the counter, and motioning for Cooper to follow, headed for Stearne's table.

Without waiting to be asked, he sat down and placed his glass and bottle on the table.

'Howdy,' he said. 'I understand you've been talking with a man named Ruben Byrd. It was the barkeep who told me.'

Cooper pulled another chair to the table and Stearne shot him an offensive look.

'Well, were you?' Lines went on when he received no answer. 'And don't give me the run-around with a smart answer. We've had enough of that already.'

Stearne eyed the two men. Their attitude suggested they weren't lawmen of any account. Lawmen knew that antagonizing a saloon owner didn't usually get you very far. The same applied to ranch hands and drifters. He topped up his glass to make a bit of time.

'The name sounds familiar. What's it to you?' he said.

Lines nodded. 'We've been chasing him all over Arkansas. My name's Lines and his is Cooper.'

'How'd you do. But I didn't ask for an introduction. I asked why you wanted to know.'

'He's the traitor who's wanted for selling out his company at Jonesboro. It was just before the War ended.' Lines answered. 'You must've heard the name.'

Stearne's face went blank for a moment, before he answered. 'Yeah, of course I've heard. Matter of fact, I was talking about him no more than an hour ago.'

'Talking about him? Who the hell with?'

'The man who bears a similar name. He said that right now it was a cross he had to bear. So it won't be him you want.'

'That's a likely goddamn tale,'

Cooper put in. 'While we're on names, what's yours?'

Stearne, breathed out slowly, trying to keep his cool, face out his lie about Ruben. 'If you were sharper-eyed, you'd have seen it already. It's over the doors you just came through. I'm Fergus Roth, the proprietor.'

Cooper grunted, helped himself to the bottle and leaned back. Trying to recall where he'd seen the man before, his eyes were boring into Stearne.

'How come you're in Vinegar Wells?' Stearne asked.

'Byrd shot a feller in Quinnel. Name of John McSwane. We figured he'd ride East.'

Stearne's face paled. McSwane! Suddenly part of the affair fell into place. Byrd was playing cat and mouse with him. If Byrd was on to McSwane . . . found him, it was a certainty he knew he was really Lester Fornell. Beads of sweat broke across his forehead, and as he lifted the Old Crow, his hand was visibly trembling.

'You're wastin' good liquor, friend,' Cooper said. 'Most of it's comin' out of your face,' he snorted.

Stearne now fought to control his voice. 'So what's got you two on his trail? Prize money?'

'No,' Lines retorted. 'I was a captain in the Volunteers. Byrd's got to pay for the soldiers he betrayed . . . the men who were slaughtered by Buckley's Runners.'

Stearne poured the last of the bourbon. He swamped the glass, forced a sickly smile as he looked at Cooper. The ex-sergeant was still trying to place him, and Stearne knew it.

'If you know he's here in town, why don't you just go for him? What's it got to do with me?' Stearne asked apprehensively.

'Your goddamn sheriff reckons Byrd's his prisoner,' Lines answered back. 'He says he knows who and what he is. He reckons he's on some sort of long leash . . . a bail while he digs up the real traitor. He's even

159

given him two days to do it.'

The information was too much for Stearne . . . too near. He coughed, spluttered as his mouthful of bourbon went down.

'I'm getting too old for this stuff,' he said. He dug for his handkerchief to wipe his mouth. 'And you still haven't said what it's got to do with me.'

'You and him were sitting right here. Real neighbourly like. He must have told you something,' Lines accused.

'If it was him, he might have done. But you don't get far in this business without knowing when to keep your mouth shut. Some of my customers rely on me not telling every Tom, Dick an' Harry who comes through the door, their business. What's more, why should I know any better than to believe him?' Stearne said.

'So it was Byrd, and you did . . . believe him,' Lines suggested.

Stearne nodded slowly. 'Likewise, if I was to believe *you two*, we could be helping each other.'

'And how's that?'

'You both look like easy money would be acceptable. So, I'll make a proposition,' Stearne began, warming a little to his idea. 'I want rid of Byrd, but it's for a different reason. It's a lady, and Byrd's crowding me.'

'You said *reasons*, and that's hardly one. What else?' Lines wanted to know.

'I've been wanting to develop my business. But I need a couple of good men to help me do it. Men who can take care of things now and again.'

Cooper sat forward in his chair. 'That usually means puttin' a bullet in someone,' he said. 'Who you got in mind?'

'Jasper. George Jasper.'

'The sheriff? You're asking us to take care of the town sheriff?' Lines queried.

Stearne took a quick, furtive look around him. 'Christ, keep your voice down,' he spluttered. 'It's taken me months to give this place eyes an' ears.'

Lines looked questioningly across to Cooper. But Cooper just shrugged and

Lines glanced back to Stearne.

'What's your problem?' the ex-captain asked.

'It's yours . . . your problem,' Stearne replied. 'You've next to no chance of gettin' that reward while Jasper's got Byrd under his wing.'

'You're not interested in what we're after. What's your beef with Jasper?'

'General. Very soon there's goin' to be rich pickin's in this town. An' with a sheriff more sympathetic to my needs . . . ' Stearne left the implication hanging. 'I reckon an ex-army officer would fit my staff requirement,' he said.

Lines returned a tired smile. 'I don't know what makes you think I'd be sympathetic to the likes o' you, Stearne. And you're taking a hell of a risk here.'

Stearne shook his head. 'This is where I don't make that sort of mistake. You've not tracked down Byrd because of any army doctrine. And you're not going to let any town sheriff come between you and a barn load of cash. What do you say?'

'Byrd first,' Cooper growled. 'He's the reason I've worn my goddamn butt out.'

'I can arrange that ... for a consideration of course. Let's say half.'

Lines grunted, his eyes flashed angrily. 'Let's say a third.'

Stearne was untroubled by Lines's anger. 'It's half, or you ride back to where you've come from, with nothing,' he offered. 'Without my help, you'll be eating worms.'

Lines simmered down. He knew that Stearne was right. While Jasper had Byrd, him and Cooper had nothing to do and nowhere to go.

'What's your plan?' he grunted.

Stearne gave a lean grin of satisfaction and reached for Lines's bottle. He poured two of his own house whiskies for Lines and Cooper, and sat back in his chair. 'You leave that to me. What you don't know, you don't suffer over, eh, Captain?'

In the edgy silence that followed,

Stearne inspected his fingernails, flicked imaginary dust from the lapels of his jacket. It was as though he'd been contaminated in some way. 'What I can tell you is that this territory's opening up, and a lot of new money's coming this way,' he said eventually. 'Bullion too . . . loads of it. That's what I'm hoping will sway your thinking.'

'Yeah? And how's that?' Lines asked, looking for the angle.

'I know how and when it arrives. You come in with me, and the reward money for Ruben Byrd is peppercorn.'

All thought of Byrd was forgotten for the moment, and Lines nodded. He raised his glass and swallowed in agreement. Beside him, Cooper was about do the same, but suddenly stopped. He looked hard at Stearne then cursed, placing his own glass back on the table.

'Your name's not Stearne,' he calmly accused. 'It's Fornell. Lester Fornell.'

10

Ex-sergeant Cooper's statement was so unexpected, that Fergus Stearne sat stunned, his face draining of colour.

'You're the gutless, lay-about private called Fornell. Another someone we thought was dead,' Cooper continued.

Stearne shook his head slowly, as though he wasn't believing what Cooper was saying. Lines's features tightened as the reality dawned. He stared first at Cooper then back at Stearne.

'You had a crony named John McSwane,' he said. 'And he was the man Byrd shot dead in Quinnel. Except he really was McSwane. We saw him.'

Cooper turned to Lines. 'Looks like we were wrong, Cap'n. It was McSwane and this horse apple sitting here. McSwane panicked when he saw Byrd, an' spilled his guts. Huh, in more ways than one.'

'Yeah, he did that all right. And Byrd

always said he was innocent. What you got to say to that, Stearne, or Fornell, or whatever your goddamn name is?' Lines's old arrogance had crept back. He was on the front foot again; his voice hardened.

Stearne helped himself to more of his house whiskey. He swallowed in one gulp, hoping to take the rising fear down with it. 'You're making a big mistake.'

'No, you've done that. I never forget a face. In your case, it's both of 'em, you son-of-a-bitch.' As Cooper spat his livid words, he reached for the Colt hanging at his side.

But Lines was alert to the situation. With a fast arm movement, he chopped hard at Cooper's wrist. 'No, Coop,' he rasped. 'You kill him, and the barman kills you. Think about it.'

As Cooper's gun clunked on the floor, some of the saloon's customers turned their heads towards the three men. Behind the bar, Harry's fingers loosened on the triggers of the scatter-gun he held below the counter.

Stearne got to his feet and, gaining control of himself, spoke out for those nearby to hear. 'Local misunderstanding. Happens sometimes ... comes with the territory,' he said by way of excuse for the commotion. He turned to Lines and Cooper. 'Let's go somewhere more private. See if we can't find a way through this problem.'

Stearne's words reassured his clientele, and as he walked towards one of two, snug and private entertaining rooms at the rear of the saloon, Lines followed him. But from behind the bar, Harry wasn't completely taken in. As Cooper leaned down to pick up his Colt, the two men exchanged a chilly look.

As they passed the back of the bar, Stearne's mind was racing. He would have taken them upstairs, but he knew there was still a body spread across the floor of his office. He was in deep trouble now, and he had to come up with a quick way out. The two men behind him wouldn't think twice about killing for money. His mind cleared for a moment as he saw the long shot. He pulled aside a thick, heavy drape, stepped into a small enclosed area that revealed a panelled door ahead of them. He dug into his waistcoat pocket for the key, stiffening as Lines's Colt jabbed sharply into his kidneys. The sound of the hammer being cocked was dulled and threatening inside the close space.

'What are you up to?' Lines growled.

'The door's locked,' Stearne said. There was little trace of emotion in his voice, but his heart was set to jump through his chest.

'This is good,' Cooper snorted, letting the big drape fall closed behind them. 'We've got our man an' that irksome sheriff's got his. Hah, he can't stop us.'

Stearne had opened the door and, with Lines's gun still rammed into the small of his back, he walked into the near darkness ahead of him, found a match and lit an oil lamp.

Cooper waited while light filled more of the rich-looking den, then he pushed the door to, behind him. 'Couldn't have found yourself a nicer place to die,' he said with menace.

Stearne glanced at the one-time sergeant and shuddered. Knowing the reward would be paid for his capture, dead or alive, he wondered if he'd just stepped into his own tomb.

'Listen, fellers,' he said eagerly. 'So, what if I am Lester Fornell, and I did renege at Jonesboro? Eh, so what? It doesn't change anything. You kill me, you only get $1,000. And what's more, you'll have to prove who I'm supposed to have been. That won't be as easy as you think.'

Lines pushed his Colt back into his holster. 'We're listening,' he said.

'You kill me, how are you going to convince the army? You reckon Byrd's going to help you?'

'Yeah, he'll help,' Cooper said. 'Even if he don't, his neck'll still get stretched.'

'But how does it prove anything?' Stearne asked. 'You've seen McSwane. It'll be my word against that of a goddamn salted stiff. All you can pin on me is desertion. And there's been an amnesty on that since the war ended.'

Lines's expression had clouded over. 'Put your iron away, Coop. He's right. We need proof he sold information to the enemy, and we don't have it.'

Stearne sat down, breathed in and out deeply. 'Back to square one, boys,' he said. 'Nothin's changed. We hand over Byrd, the same as before.'

'We can prove this cur did it easy enough,' Cooper growled. 'Where'd he get the brass to buy this place? A private's pay wouldn't even buy a spit bowl.'

'True.' Lines nodded in agreement. 'If needs be, old John Buckley could certainly identify the man who betrayed us. I heard he was settled somewhere outside of Springfield.'

Lines walked across the room to a side table, lifted a brandy decanter.

He held the neck to his mouth and took a good pull. He licked his lips appreciatively and carefully replaced the decanter, looked up at the sweating grey face of Stearne.

'You look like someone's just stepped on your grave,' he said. 'Get yourself back to the living. I've got it figured. We'll do as you say. But from now on we're partners . . . straight down the middle.' Lines looked around the small, luxuriously furnished room. 'This is the sort of company I could fit right into. What do you reckon, Coop?'

Cooper hadn't had the time or reason to appreciate Lines's thinking. He looked blank for a moment, then he grinned. 'Yeah. I'm stakin' this as my office,' he mused.

Stearne glowered resentfully at the two men. He was caught now, and he knew it. For the time being all he could do was go along with them.

'Now for Ruben Byrd,' Lines said. 'Tell us more of that proposition. What's your plan?'

★　★　★

Ruben was seated at a table in Annie Desmond's house. His hair was slicked down and pomaded and his face was clean shaved, but he felt uncomfortable in the linsey-woolsey shirt he'd bought at the mercantile that afternoon. Annie had seen his discomfort when he'd arrived. He looked like a young man on his first date, and she smiled to herself. But over the pea soup, the formality eased, and as the meal had gone on, a relationship had sprung up between them.

Not long after his second dish of tinned milk over tinned peaches, Ruben raised a coffee cup to his lips and sipped reflectively. As he placed the cup back in the saucer, Annie offered him a cigar.

'Any further visits, and I'll have smoked them all,' he said good humouredly.

'Then I'll buy some more.'

'Just to keep me coming?'

172

'Yes. Just to keep you coming.'

'Thanks. It's been a long time since I've had more than ten minutes not thinking about what I'm doing or where I'm going. I've enjoyed myself this evening.'

'Me too. But with those ten minutes well and truly up, we're into the right now. I'm sorry, but what happened this afternoon? Did you find out anything?'

'I think so, yes. I reckon you were right about your husband. He was blackmailing Fergus Stearne, I'll swear to it. And that means that Stearne is the man I'm after. How I'm going to get him to talk, though, is another matter. Maybe I'll just have to kill him.'

'Hmm, and maybe. Maybes aren't flying this time of year,' Annie said wryly. 'Either way, you'll have to get him into the open. How are you going to do that?'

'I don't know. I wish I'd put a bullet into McSwane's leg instead of his gut. He could've told the tale.'

'With him still alive, you'd have had

twice the battle trying to figure out which of the two you were after. Besides, you wouldn't have met me, would you?'

Ruben nodded. 'That's true.'

'What does the sheriff think?'

'He's got enough on his plate with the stage hold-up. And there's the two army fellers to keep an eye on.'

'What army fellers? Who are you talking about?' Annie asked anxiously.

'The pair who've come looking for me. According to George, they're a couple of real Jack Nasty characters. He told them I was under bail or something, and for them to lay off. But ... ' Ruben left the sentence unfinished. With her obvious liking for him, he'd meant to explain in a more careful way. 'You'd have to be pretty hard-nosed to go for someone who's under the personal protection of a town sheriff. To disregard that must carry dire consequences,' he added hurriedly, attempting to lessen the worry.

'So two armed soldiers have come to

174

gun you down?' Annie said.

Ruben got up from his chair and walked to the window, looked out towards the night. 'Not if I stay in the open,' he replied with a tight, uncertain smile.

Accepting the realness of the situation, Annie remained taut and doubtful. She got up from the table and smoothed down the creases of her dress. Her raven hair fell straight to her shoulders, framing her face and dark misty eyes.

'I know it's none of my business, but I don't want you to get hurt,' she said, stepping closer. 'A few days ago I wouldn't have known . . . it wouldn't have mattered. But now it does. Do you know what I'm trying to say?'

Ruben turned and looked at her, the smile warming. 'Of course I do. You knew I did before you asked. I've come this far, Annie, I reckon I'll see it through. And if you think about it, these fellers might just put the fear of God into Stearne. All they want is the turncoat and the reward money that goes with it. If he gives something away and they start to suspect him, then he's finished.'

Ruben took Annie's arm, walked her from the window. 'Let's talk about something else, now . . . like how you prepared such a spread when you're only a few hours back from Beaver Lakes.'

Annie was about to explain how she'd had neighbourly help, when a double rap sounded on the front door. She turned and looked at Ruben, consternation creasing her features.

'Who the . . . ?' she said, and stepped into the hallway.

Ruben quickly drew his Colt from his gun-belt that was coiled on top of a chest of drawers. He cocked the hammer, stood close against the wall to one side of the doorway. He heard the door open, held his breath for a moment to listen for a voice, but none came.

'There's no one here,' Annie said a

few moments later, after taking a look and pushing the door back to.

Ruben cursed silently. *Well, there goddamn was*, he thought, moving into the doorway.

'But someone left this,' Annie was holding an envelope that she'd picked up. 'It's for you . . . Ruben Byrd.'

Ruben replaced his Colt, decided to put his gun belt back on. He took the envelope and ran his thumb up inside the closing fold. He pulled out a single sheet of paper, read it quickly and handed it back to Annie.

'Looks like the devil we speak of has something on his mind,' he said.

Annie shook her head slowly as she read. ''Byrd, I've got information. I know who you're after and can help. Meet me at the stables at 10 tonight. Fergus Stearne.' He must think you're some sort of half-wit to fall for that,' she added.

Ruben looked at the clock on the mantelshelf. It was almost 9.30. He had half an hour. 'I've got to go, Annie. I can't risk all these months just because I'm not keen on the *rendezvous*.'

Annie's shoulders dropped with sadness. 'Then go and get the sheriff. Take him with you.'

'Can't. There might be something needs doing that isn't strictly legal. You know what a stickler George can be.' Ruben leaned forward and pressed his lips to her forehead. She wrapped her arms about him, and squeezed emotionally. He eased her off to arm's length, smiling silent curses as he saw the hurt in her dark eyes. But he let go of her, reached for his hat and strode to the door.

'Ruben, please . . . ' she started to say, the pleading obvious in her voice.

'I'm coming back,' he said. 'Where I come from, it's said that if a young lady serenades a man with soup and cigars, there's a lot more on offer.' Without giving any time for a reply, he closed the door and headed out for his horse.

Annie went immediately back into the parlour. She reached for the box of cigars and with a fast wave of her arm, sent them crashing across the room. 'What's the goddamn point?' she shouted. A few minutes later, she'd donned a shawl, and was heading determinedly for George Jasper's office.

11

The moon stole out from behind the clouds, and silvery light mantled the town. At the far end of the main street, Ruben was leaning forward in the saddle. In the distance he heard the troubled bark of a dog, then a voice shouting for it to keep quiet. Muffled sounds drifted from the saloon. *Huh, you haven't brought them all with you then*, he thought, wondering if Stearne was on his own. A moment later, he turned his concentration on the large corral looming out of the darkness ahead of him. He eased his Colt in the holster, heeling the roan to continue its steady walk.

The town's stables were large. Horse boxes were arranged along the rear end of the yard. To his left was a farrier's shop and to the right, small, timbered buildings which were the stores and tool and harness sheds. He walked the roan into the middle of the yard and slipped from the saddle.

'Byrd. I'm over here,' Stearne called.

If it's a trap, he's sprung the first part, Ruben thought, turning in the direction of the man's voice.

With reins in one hand, the other hanging close to his Colt, Ruben walked slowly towards the saloon keeper. 'This is a bit dramatic, Stearne. Something wrong with the Applejack?' he said calmly.

Stearne was standing in deeper shadow beside one of the sheds. 'It's better here,' he replied. 'I don't always want folk to know my business.'

Ruben paused. He eased the Colt from is holster and drew back the hammer. 'I'm an exception, Stearne. I'll talk where I can see you, proper.'

'It's not talk, Byrd. There's something here I want you to see.'

'Yeah, I bet. To use words you understand . . . no dice,' Ruben snapped. 'You've already broken up my evening with Annie

Desmond, so get into the open, goddamn-it.' Ruben thought the mention of Annie would aggravate Stearne enough to bring him out.

It wasn't just the feeling of not being alone that made Ruben's nerves tighten. It was the slight sound somewhere behind him. He shivered at his gut feeling, turning quickly as sweat broke between his shoulder blades. He went into a crouch, but it was too late to stop the vicious blow on the side of his head. As the pain and darkness gripped him, he knew Annie was right. *Me. I'm the sort of half-wit who'd fall . . .* , he was thinking as he crumpled unconscious into the hard-packed dirt of the yard.

★   ★   ★

When Ruben stirred he found himself tied hand and foot. He rolled on to his shoulder and raised himself from the floor, wincing at the pain rushing backwards and forwards in his skull.

182

There was low, yellow light from an oil lamp and he closed his eyes, opened them again to look around him. A plush carpet was crumpled underneath him, and he guessed he must be somewhere in Stearne's saloon. Attempting to get himself into a kneeling position, he gritted his teeth, drew his legs into his chest.

As he took a shallow breath, he heard voices filtering through the nearest wall. He managed to huddle against the ornately papered wall and lean his head in close. The voices were low, but whoever was talking didn't sound like they were concerned at being over-heard.

'Well, I think we should finish him off now,' a voice came through the wall.

'No, Coop. If I live to be a hundred, I don't want to see any more preserved corpses, let alone tote one halfway across the country. Besides, we'll likely have to tangle with that mule-headed lawman,' someone else said.

Ruben didn't recognize either voice.

He pressed the knuckles of both his hands into the floor for more support, but holding his breath and straining to hear, it took all his strength to hold his head up.

'He's right. It'll be easier for you to get him out of town alive. I'm not the only one who's got his lookouts.' Now it was Fergus Stearne doing the speaking.

'So what about the sheriff, Cap'n? We could quieten him before we go?'

'That can wait until you come back,' Stearne said. 'Byrd and my proposal aren't rightly related. Besides, I can't set up the town if Jasper's dead and you two have gone to Texas. And I need your help installing my man in the law office.'

To Ruben, the rest of the talking sounded woolly. But he'd learned enough. The two men with Stearne were evidently the army men, and they'd plotted together. What Ruben didn't understand was their connection with Stearne. They'd only ridden in that afternoon, so Stearne had moved real fast.

The voices continued in the next room, but Ruben was more queasy and hurting from the crack across his head. He sunk back to the floor in fatigue, watched the light from the lamp get dimmer as he drifted into blackness again.

$\star$ $\star$ $\star$

Annie Desmond wasn't more than five minutes behind Ruben when she left her house. As she ran towards the centre of town, and George Jasper's office, she snatched angrily at the woollen shawl about her shoulders.

As she passed the seats under the cottonwood, she looked further along the street. She saw the twin oil lamps outside the sheriff's office and jailhouse were lit, and she quickened her step. One or two townsfolk watched her as she hurried along the boardwalk. They shared inquisitive glances, a negative

185

word, before continuing with their business.

At the jailhouse, Annie sighed. She could see the interior lamps inside were trimmed down. She tried the door, but it was locked as she guessed it would be. She anxiously stepped one way then the other, looking around, hoping she might see Jasper returning.

'Mrs Desmond. What in blue blazes are you up to at this hour?' the town blacksmith inquired as he stepped up from the street.

'I'm looking for the sheriff,' Annie said anxiously. 'I don't suppose you know where he is, do you?'

'Happen I do, ma'am. Fact, could be the only one who does. He rode out a few hours ago. Can't be far. Said he'd be back by morning.'

Annie nodded her thanks, ground her teeth in frustration. Fighting to control her disappointment and helplessness, she crossed the street to the opposite boardwalk. She'd known Ruben was walking into a trap, to her way of thinking, there was nothing else it was ever going to be.

Suddenly she paused, half-turned towards the store window beside her. Three men were approaching from the corral end of town. Pulling the shawl more securely about her, she hastened to the side alley of the Applejack Room. She knew the men were headed her way because she was sure one of them was Fergus Stearne. Making sure that she wasn't seen by anyone, she stepped into the alley, stood close to the front corner and waited. She was standing in deep shadow, hoping that the men would enter the saloon, come no further along the street.

Annie had only just realized she was within fifty or sixty feet of where her husband had been shot, when the advancing men stopped outside the ornate doors of the saloon. She was close enough to hear their conversation before they went inside.

'Let's not look like a guilty party,' said Stearne.

'Huh, I'm sure you're real good at that,' a low voice replied. 'But it don't worry us. By the time your goddamn sheriff discovers he's got himself a bail jumper, we'll be lookin' to the risin' sun . . . well out of his thoughts, an' his reach.'

Annie's heart immediately thumped harder. She knew it was Ruben they were talking about.

'Why not go tonight . . . now?' she heard Stearne ask.

'Because I'm not making a cold camp on the trail,' another voice said. 'Nothing much is going to happen in the next few hours. So let's have a drink or two on the house.'

A wedge of light cut across the boardwalk and into the street as the three men entered the saloon. The doors swung shut, and Annie stood shocked and unmoving with her back to the clap-boarded wall. She held her hand hard against her chest to try and restrain the pounding of her heart, then around her mouth to stop herself screaming. *Dumb, fool-headed man,* she thought in her anger. *He wasn't ever going to listen.* She didn't know where Ruben might be, what had happened to him, what she could do. Her head was a whirl of irrational ideas, but she had heard where they were taking him, and when.

More footsteps sounded from the boardwalk, and she stepped away from the wall, backing further into the alleyway. At the rear of the saloon, she forced herself not to look where she knew her husband's body must have lain less than a month ago. She turned left, running along the backs of the buildings, past sheds and stores and trash cans until she emerged from where she could make it back to her house without being seen.

By the time she got home, Annie was winded, wheezing with distress as she staggered to her front door. Inside the house, she ran to the parlour, giving way to her emotions as she paced around the room.

After five minutes of miserable hurt, she wiped her hair from her face and started to wonder about her feelings for Ruben. In less than a full day, she was reacting as though he'd become the grubstake of her life. She shook her head in confusion, had a reflective look at the photographs on the mantelshelf.

'So, perhaps he has,' she muttered. 'And I'd best do something about it.'

Quickly, but more calmly, she walked to her bedroom, fingering the buttons on her dress as she went. It took her less than five minutes to change into a more appropriate outfit, adequate time for her to decide what she was going to do next.

She may not be sixteen any more, but she was enamoured, she recognized. She smiled weakly at her seeming foolishness, then hollowly, as she considered the implications of what Fergus Stearne had said. Now she realized he'd been speaking to the hard-bit army men who Ruben said had come looking for him.

She reached into the back of her wardrobe and drew out the Yellowboy carbine. Her husband had bought it for her, had even tried to teach her how to use it. But, other than one short practice on the other side of the river, well outside of town, she never had. He'd said it was essential for her protection when he wasn't around. She'd maintained that if she needed a rifle to protect her in Vinegar Wells, then she wouldn't be staying to find out why. But now it was all different. She opened and closed the trigger lever to a push a bullet into the firing chamber, hoped it was all she would have to do this side of firing it.

Within half an hour she had been to the livery stable, had a rimrock mare saddled up and was riding east.

12

The three riders weren't far beyond where the Bitter River curled in a loop around the outskirts of town.

Morgan Lines was aware that Ruben was looking at him with open hostility.

'Whatever it is, forget it, Byrd,' he said. 'You've been on borrowed time since the day you broke out of Fort Clinton. It's true what they say about an ill wind, though. You've changed our luck. What do you reckon, Coop?'

Cooper, unshaven and bleary-eyed in the pale light of dawn, coughed. 'Yeah, Cap'n. We pick up a grand as well as a share in a saloon when we return. An' then whatever else that swellhead's got in mind.'

Ruben tried to ignore their banter. His head still ached from the blow he'd received. But it was sharp and fixed, no debilitating clash inside his skull.

Twisting his hands in the rope that bound them, he grabbed the pommel between his fingers and looked straight ahead.

The ex-sergeant spat down into the dust, wiped a greasy sleeve across his chin.

'What about the sheriff, Cap'n? They said he'd be comin' back this mornin'. Reckon we might run into him . . . him into us?'

'Not unless he's riding in one big circle. He went out on the other side of town.'

Ruben cursed silently. He'd overheard that George Jasper was out of town, and he'd hoped for a long shot that their trails would meet. His shoulders dropped slightly, and he allowed himself to sag in the saddle. For the umpteenth time, he cursed himself for getting caught.

'Got a woodbine on you?' he said, turning to Lines.

Without looking up, Lines dug into his vest and pulled out a lean cheroot.

He eased his mount over to Byrd and held out his hand, dropping the smoke between the two horses as Ruben reached for it.

Ruben shook his head. 'What a waste,' he said ruefully. 'But I guess it just about sums you up.'

As Ruben prepared himself for a blow from Lines, a voice called out from a small brake of willow at the side of the trail.

'Don't move, any of you. Just stay put.'

Lines immediately turned to face the challenge. He swallowed hard as he saw Annie Desmond, her long, dark hair spilling out from under a range hat, the Yellowboy carbine pointed straight at him.

Cooper twisted around in the saddle. 'What in hell . . . ?' he started.

'You will be, if you don't do as I say,' Annie threatened.

'You'd best put that little smoke pole down, before I come an' take it from you,' he rasped.

'My husband said he won this from Billy Blackwood in a game of poker,' Annie said. 'He was told it was loaded with bullets that could blow holes in a bank door from fifty feet. You don't have to bother much with an aim . . . just pull the trigger. You want me to try it here?'

'Steady, Coop. She's strung real tight,' Lines warned.

'Yeah, real tight,' Ruben agreed. He leaned over and pulled Lines's Colt from its holster, but the ex-officer didn't take his eyes off Annie.

'And you throw down your side-arm,' Annie ordered Cooper with a menacing prod of the carbine. 'And do it now.'

But already the confrontation on top of the day's events was taking its toll. Annie's eyes were losing their sharpness and her boldness was failing under Cooper's goading, malevolent stare.

Cooper knew it, decided to press and take his chance. He lurched sideways, at the same time drawing his Colt and swinging it towards Annie.

But Annie's reflexes were hair-triggered. The carbine bucked in her hand, there was a sharp report, and a jolt shot up her arm into her shoulder.

Cooper squirmed violently in the saddle as Annie's wilful shot found a target. He let out a sound like a rebel yell, dropping his Colt as a bullet ripped into the fleshy part of his right arm.

Ruben lifted his hands from the saddle pommel. He eased the startled roan with a calming word, then told Lines to dismount. 'Get yourself over here and untie me,' he commanded.

Annie had already dismounted. She'd slipped unsteadily from the saddle and was standing over Cooper, the carbine pointing at his head. She was trembling from head to toe and Ruben saw she wasn't far from falling.

Lines considered his chances of knocking the gun from Ruben's grasp. But it was all too close and tense and he decided against it.

'You make one move and I'll shoot you dead, Cap'n,' Ruben advised. 'If I'm the man you think I am, you'll know I'm capable.' As the ropes fell from his wrists, Ruben turned his attention to Cooper.

'Get to your feet,' he snapped. 'Pick up his gun, Annie.'

Holding his shattered arm, Cooper staggered up and Ruben shoved him over to stand beside Lines.

'Take a rein off each horse,' Ruben said to Annie.

'What are you going to do?'

'Tie these two up. I'm going to hobble them by the neck. If either of them makes a threatening move, shoot,' Ruben said. 'If they get me, they certainly won't be taking you back to town.'

Ruben used one rein to bind and tie each of the men's wrists behind their backs. With the other, he fashioned a slipping coil around their necks.

'You be real careful. Pull too tight . . . try and get away from each other and you'll choke,' he warned them.

The moment Lines and Cooper were secured and Ruben backed off, Annie's strength failed her. She dropped the carbine and her legs buckled.

'I like your timing,' Ruben said. He lifted up the Yellowboy, gave an appreciative nod. 'Nice piece of ordnance.'

'Is it? I've never done anything like this before,' she said, smiling feebly in return.

'I thought I was riding to the bone house. I didn't have you down for a rifleman.'

'I'm not. I got the bit about Billy Blackwood from a dime novel in the mercantile. My eyes were actually closed when I fired.'

Ruben shook his head slowly with disbelief. 'Well, they say good luck never comes too late. I'm grateful, Annie . . . real grateful. Now, we'll head back to town. There's someone I've got a problem with.'

Cooper lifted his head and scowled.

'What about me? My arm's busted like a . . .'

Ruben walked over to the two men. 'If you were your horse, I'd put a bullet in you now,' he answered to Cooper. 'There's some shade under the trees. That's as far as my concern's going.'

'I could bleed to death,' the man moaned.

'Yeah, reckon you could. Unless the coyotes get wind. Then it'll be something else. The sheriff can collect them later,' he told Annie as he turned his back on them. 'As long as I don't forget to tell him where they are.'

Ruben put the men's Colts into Cooper's saddlebags, at the same time retrieving his own .36 Navy Colt and gun-belt. Then he swung aboard his roan.

'You're actually going to leave them here?' Annie asked uncertainly as she mounted her mare.

'You bet I am. They're not going anywhere. One of them trips, and the other one strangles. Now, unless you

199

want to stay and entertain them, let's get going.'

Ruben leaned down from the saddle, picked up the single rein from each of the ex-soldiers' mounts, then nudged his horse with his heels. With a single thought in mind, he headed determinedly back to Vinegar Wells.

★ ★ ★

George Jasper had walked from the corrals, was approaching his office when Ruben and Annie rode into town.

'Ruben? Mrs Desmond? What's up?' he asked.

'One fat goddamn lot is what,' Ruben snapped as he jumped to the ground. 'Let's get inside. I think my job's near to done.'

Jasper followed Ruben into the office. He went to his desk and threw his war bag underneath. 'Pull up a couple o' chairs. Near to done, you say?'

'Yeah. Lines and Cooper cold-cocked me last night. Let's not bother about where or how at the moment. But Fergus Stearne's in with them. This morning, they tried to get me away from town. They would have too, if Carbine Kate here hadn't been lying in wait for us.'

Jasper's eyes lifted at the unlikely incident. 'Stearne, huh? Why aren't I surprised?' he replied. 'All of a sudden, he's become answerable to more than a stage robbery.'

'That was him? Fergus Stearne?' Annie asked.

'Not one of them who did it, no. But he was sure pulling some strings. Now, give me details about last night, what happened to the pair o' you.'

13

Jasper poked around the bits and pieces on his desk top for his pipe. He studied its charred bowl for a moment, then looked up, his expression troubled as he considered Ruben's plan.

'We haven't time to come up with much else,' he accepted.

Ruben got up and turned to Annie. 'You'd better go home, Annie,' he advised. 'But this time I'm taking your advice, so there's no need to worry.'

'You were thinking that last time,' she said, but nodding in agreement. 'At least George will be there watching out.'

As the two men went off to the saloon, Annie lifted her hand in a nervous wave. 'See you in a while,' she said, then headed for the livery with the rimrock mare.

'Assuming it's open, we'll go in the

back way,' Jasper said to Ruben. 'Through the front doors might be asking for trouble.'

'Yeah, sort of,' Ruben agreed. 'I'm thinking that if he decides to deny everything, we're both back where we started.'

'Don't forget the pair o' rats you left back on the trail,' Jasper reminded him.

'Hah, if they actually were rats, they might drop him in it. But they won't. They've got stuff to lose.'

Jasper shook his head, indicated they turn into an alley. 'When I introduce them to the town's big ol' cottonwood, they'll talk. Believe me, they'll sing like canaries, Rube. It's one of the few immutable things a sheriff gets to know.'

The two men reached the end of the alley. They stopped for a moment to look and listen, then they turned left, walking their mounts on towards the Applejack.

At the back corner of the saloon, Ruben hitched his roan to a fence rail, went straight to the back door of the building. He tried the handle, allowing himself a short, tight grin when it moved and the door opened. 'Trusting son-of-a-bitch. How wrong can they be?' he muttered.

Jasper came up behind him. 'Why not the back stairs?' he whispered.

'Because we don't know for sure he's up there. If he's at the bar, well and good. If not, then we'll go on up. There's a narrow flight of steps that leads from outside the bar's stockroom up to the first floor landing. Lord knows what it's for, but we'll use it. Either way, we'll find somewhere for you to listen in. I did.'

Easing aside one of the heavy drapes that flanked the bar, Ruben took a look around the saloon. Harry the barman was being kept busy, but Stearne didn't appear to be at his usual table or anywhere else in the large room.

Ruben indicated to Jasper that it was clear, that they should take the steps up to the landing and Stearne's private offices. Testing each tread carefully, he led the way.

'You sure he's here?' Jasper asked quietly when they'd reached the top.

'Well, he's not down there,' Ruben said. 'You can hole up in the corner room along here. It's next to Stearne's. Find yourself a place to listen. If you don't hear anything, just pretend you did when you come busting in.'

At a nod from Ruben, Jasper peered into the dark interior, cautiously let himself into the room. He held his Colt across his chest and leaned against the adjoining wall.

Ruben took a couple of deep breaths. He looked about him, across the landing area to the broad main staircase. Satisfied there was no one else around, he stepped forward and confronted Stearne's door. He drew back the hammer of his Colt, in one continuous movement, gripped the door handle turned it and pushed the door open.

Fergus Stearne was standing behind

his large desk. His opened his mouth to protest at the rude intrusion, then his jaw fell, and his eyes bulged as Ruben came towards him.

'I know,' Ruben started. 'You weren't expecting to see me again. You're thinking, *he's a dead man.*'

'How? Where's Lines? Where's Cooper?' Stearne faltered.

'Somewhere on the trail outside of town, trussed up like a brace of Thanksgiving turkeys. Now, Stearne, or should I say, Fornell, let's do some talking.'

Stearne closed his eyes for moment as he thought. 'Well, Mr Ruben Byrd. It seems you can keep a secret as well as anyone else. What was all that chummy chat nonsense when you came into town? Why not come straight out with what you had?'

'John McSwane.'

'Ah, of course. I heard about what happened. I certainly picked a loser there for a partner.' Stearne smiled grimly at the memory of McSwane.

'Still, he did allow me to keep all those dollars.'

Ruben bunched the fingers of both hands in anger and frustration. In appearance, Stearne certainly looked the part of a respectable and successful businessman. What flawed the look were the callous eyes.

'You'll allow the accused man a drink?' he said.

Ruben nodded. 'Yeah, one for the road to George Jasper's jail. You're going to tell him the story.'

'I said accused, not guilty,' Stearne smirked. 'Me telling you is one thing. Proving it's another. I'll deny everything. It'll never get to court.'

'And Lines and Cooper?'

'You think either one of them is going to put their head in a noose? No, they won't talk, Byrd. You're stymied.'

Ruben stared contemptuously as Stearne poured himself a large whiskey.

'You don't look like the sort of man who's taken a beating recently, Stearne,' he said. 'Think about it. You can confess all in reasonable comfort, *or* looking like a mutton chop *and* in a lot of pain. You'll talk either way. I'm giving you the choice.'

The saloon owner was disturbed by Ruben's anger. He took a gulp of his whiskey.

'Knocking me about won't get you what you want,' he replied. 'I'll recover, and when I do, the town's open for me again. I've built myself up too well to let you or that goddamn sheriff stop me.'

'For chris'sake, Stearne, I'm not going to knock you about,' Rube exploded. 'For what's happened to me, you'll be crippled for life. And that building you've done doesn't amount to a hill of beans, anymore. Your false-front days are over.'

'Listen, Byrd. Who the hell do you think was behind that Black Rock stage hold-up? If it hadn't have been for someone else's misjudgement, I'd have my hands on the whole shipment. But people like me learn quickly from mistakes, and there'll be more coming.'

Stearne topped up his glass, took another sip. 'Besides, it's your word against three. And who's going to believe a suspected traitor? The worst of the worst.'

'You think it's all figured out, Stearne. But there's a couple of small things you've overlooked.'

Stearne tilted his head in mock concern. 'Out of interest, what are they? I haven't had to worry about small things for a while.'

'You'll worry about this. How do you think I got away from your army boys? Who helped me . . . and saw you arrange the whole thing? Who was waiting on the trail as we rode by?'

'Hmm. I can guess. You said a couple of things. What else you got?' Stearne still sounded confident, but it was waning as Ruben continued.

'I've got George Jasper on my side. He's not going to like the idea of you taking over the town. Even less about the bit about you being smarter than him.'

'What's he going to do about it? He knows nothing.'

'He'll be working on that right now. You can ask him yourself. These walls have ears, Stearne, and he's been listening to every mean, goddamn word you've just said. You've talked yourself into that noose.'

Stearne dropped the whiskey glass. It crashed on to the desk and he made a quick sideways move to pick it up. But his hand dived into his shoulder holster to draw his hideout gun.

Ruben shook his head intolerantly. 'I've just told you. Sheriff Jasper was standing behind that wall. Now he's about to kick his way in here.'

In two minds, Stearne looked from Ruben to the door. 'Might as well drop for a sheep then,' he rasped. 'At least you won't be seeing him.'

That was the moment the door of the office flew open and Jasper strode in. He was ready for what confronted him and without pause his Colt belched flame. The hideout gun was smashed from Stearne's hand, and as he spun away, Ruben threw one arm tight around his neck, the other pushing against the back of his head.

'I've got reasons to snap you, Stearne. I'm that goddamn close,' he snarled.

Stearne raised the broken fingers of his right hand, offered a muffled grunt of submission.

Ruben let him go, swung and pushed him into the big chair beside the desk. 'Did you hear what was said?' he asked of Jasper.

'Most of it . . . enough anyway,' Jasper said. 'Worked out better than we hoped.'

'Another second or two and it wouldn't have,' Ruben answered back. 'How about the coach robbery?'

Jasper nodded. 'Yeah. I sort of had it figured that way. We found the body of an owl hoot with a .44 rifle bullet in him. According to the doc, though, he was carrying another smaller one in his gut. One that would probably have killed him anyway.'

The sheriff turned and faced Stearne. 'Big mistake, Stearne ... placing unnecessary evidence like that. You shot a man who was already dead.' Jasper extracted a small lead bullet from his vest pocket, held it up for them to see. 'With this,' he added decisively.

Ruben looked down at Stearne, saw the man's facial muscles twitch savagely.

'Get your hat. We're leaving,' Jasper said.

At the bottom of the main staircase, the Applejack's cleaners were just finishing their chores. Harry the barman's face was a mask of curiosity. All of them stopped working, watched impassively as Stearne was escorted past them, directly to the main doors.

'Somethin' caught up with him?' Harry asked.

'Yeah, the law,' Jasper rasped back. 'I reckon we've solved the bank robbery.'

Ruben flexed the tiredness out of his shoulders, watched as the saloon swampers downed gear and followed on. He knew the news would be all over town before they had time to reach the jail.

Along the main street, one woman singled herself out. She was the widow of the dead stagecoach driver. As they passed her by, Jasper paused and looked down at her from the boardwalk. Her eyes were wintry cold, emotionless.

'When's the hanging?' she asked in a low, cracking voice.

'Soon. Meantime, if you want to spit or something, that's OK,' Jasper answered a moment later, but the woman had already turned away.

'Why don't we string him up now?' someone called.

Jasper turned and glared back at the group. 'Cause while I'm sheriff, this isn't a goddamn lynch town, that's why,' he railed at them. 'Now break it up, move along.'

Ruben watched Stearne at the exchange of affecting words. Gone was the self-assured swagger. The man was beginning to tremble and sweat beaded his top lip. He took sharp, shallow breaths, stared with fearful eyes at the people who had been his customers and friends.

'Now you know what it feels like. Try and imagine it if you're innocent,' Ruben said. 'But you're lucky. It'll end soon after they slip the noose over your head.'

Jasper waved them into the jailhouse. Without wasting any time on arrest and booking procedures, he locked Stearne in one of the double cells. Then he slumped in his chair and threw the keys on his desk.

'I guess there's more than a few who'd say to throw those away,' he said, tiredly. He opened a desk drawer and took out a small, flat bottle of French brandy, studied the label. 'I'm pleased for you, Rube,' he said. 'I don't mind admitting, when you rode in here, I considered locking you up and sending for the army. But that was before I let personal feelings interfere. I guess I've

214

learned something.'

Ruben nodded. 'Goes for me too, George,' he replied, looking towards the cells. 'It's a shame hangings are only one-time.'

Jasper slowly drew the cork from the whiskey, leaned back and looked at his friend. 'I'd offer you a glass, but I haven't got one,' he said with a wry smile.

Ruben held up his hand in an OK gesture. 'I'll go and tell Annie,' he said. 'That is, if she isn't on armed guard outside the door. Then I'll come back . . . take you out to where I left Lines and Cooper.'

'OK, Rube. I've some paperwork to do on all this. And from what you say, those two aren't going anywhere.'

'What will they get?'

Jasper took a long satisfying pull from the bottle, thought for a moment. 'Attempted murder, kidnapping, accessory after the fact? They'll probably be standing alongside Stearne.'

Ruben smiled grimly and headed for

the door. He didn't think Jasper was right in his summation. But he thought the man's heart was in the right place.

14

The old man twisted around in the seat of the buck wagon and looked at his two passengers. 'Ain't you fellers goin' to the jailhouse to report what happened?' he asked.

'We've other stuff to take care of,' Morgan Lines growled. 'Thanks for the ride. Just drop us off here.'

'Well, Sheriff Jasper don't appreciate dry-gulchers. He'll sure as hell want to know about this. An' I'd get that arm o' yours looked at by the doc, if I was you,' he said to Cooper.

'Well, you're not,' Cooper snapped back. He'd had Lines use one of the reins that bound his wrists to strap his right arm right against his chest.

'Suit yourself,' the old hoe-man said.

He watched as Cooper climbed awkwardly to the ground. As Lines followed he shrugged, flicked the reins for his horse to move on along the main street.

'Silly ol' fool. You think he swallowed our story of bein' held up an' robbed?' Cooper said.

'Yeah. It's a story that'll earn him a beer or two. Either that, or he's forgotten us already. Come on, we need guns *and* horses.'

'What about Stearne?'

'Byrd will have the law breathing down his neck by now. We've got to get to him first in case Jasper gets him to mouth off.'

Cooper shot Lines a frosty stare, then looked along the street. 'I suppose a snort's out o' the question? Don't need two hands to lift a goddamn glass.'

Lines didn't respond. Ahead of them a small crowd was gathering, and he signalled caution as they continued along the boardwalk.

'Let's hear that again, Tom. An' not so fast this time,' one of the men was saying.

'Stearne's under lock an' key. Apparently, he was behind the stage hold-up . . . the organ grinder. An' that ain't all. It was him who gunned down Drew Desmond behind his own saloon.'

As the townsfolk pressed around the mercantile owner, Lines nudged Cooper off the street into a side-alley.

'Jasper's already jailed him,' he rasped angrily. 'We'll have to break him out. Goddamnit.'

'Why not leave him there? They'll pin the lot on him.'

Lines scowled. 'I've said it once, Coop, I'll say it again. I haven't come this far for nothing. I want that money.'

'Well, how you goin' to get it now?'

'We spring him. How difficult can it be? He'll be glad to cough up when he's back in fresh air. What he does . . . where he goes after that is his business.'

'Without guns? Where'd you reckon on gettin' one . . . two even? An' soon. I don't like bein' in danger.'

'Where are guns likely to be found in

a peaceable town like this?'

'The sheriff's office.'

'Yeah. Everything we need in one place. He'll have confiscations locked in a drawer. Maybe a couple hanging up, as well as his own. So that's where we're going, Coop. To jail.'

Cooper shrugged. 'How'd we get to him?' he asked. 'The way things are, he's not likely to welcome us in.'

'I know. But we're not exactly paying him a courtesy call.'

The two men turned to the right. They were walking cautiously along the back alleys in the direction of the jailhouse, when Lines stopped.

'It's not the outcome I'd planned, Coop, but we're not finished,' he said. 'Remember, a man surprised is half beat. So we won't knock.'

'What happens when we're inside?'

'If the sheriff's not talking, and no one sees us, they'll assume Stearne jumped him and escaped.'

'What about us?'

'The oldster will say how he found us

out on the trail, and we'll tell the truth
. . . say it was Byrd. Don't forget, as far
as the army's concerned, he's still the
traitor. We get rid of him, then it's the
gravy run for both of us.'

During the War, Cooper had roughed
his way in and out of many a tight
corner. But now there was a doubt. It
was all a bit speculative for the
one-time private. 'But Stearne's wanted
for the stage job,' he said.

'I'll handle that,' Lines replied a tad
impatiently. 'If the town suspects it's us,
all well and good. They'll probably
rustle up another reward. Meantime,
we'll have Stearne's cash, Byrd's body
and be in the clear.'

At last the plan sank in and Cooper
contrived a sheepish grin. 'Yeah. Now I
can see how you got them pips, Cap'n,'
he said.

The flattering remark was ignored,
and Lines waved Cooper on. Sneaking
along the back wall, he led the way until
they reached the rear of the jail-house.
He inched forward, towards the main

street, stopping to kneel where he could see under the blind of the narrow, side window.

He saw that George Jasper was at his desk, occupied with legal paperwork. Within easy reach was a .44 Colt. A shoulder holster was hanging from a hat stand, and the rifle rack appeared to be unlocked. He stood up, looked hard at Cooper. 'Let's do it,' he said.

The two men slipped further along the building's side wall, then on to the boardwalk at the main street.

'Stay right here. I'll call for you,' Lines said. Looking calm, he stepped up to the jailhouse door and turned the handle. He pushed the door open and quickly stepped inside.

Taken by surprise, Jasper flinched. He looked up from his work and Lines instantly held out his hand to indicate that he should keep still, no fuss.

'Go for that gun and a lady's going to die,' he threatened. 'It's a threat unworthy of an officer and a gentleman, but right this moment, I'm desperate.'

'Who are you talking about?' Jasper demanded.

'You'll find out if I don't appear at your front window within the next ten seconds.'

Jasper stared at the window then the door. Then he inched his hand away from the Colt.

Lines grabbed it. 'Get in here, Coop,' he shouted.

'What the hell's going on?' Jasper rasped. 'Who are you holding out there?'

'No one,' Lines said, and pressed the barrel of the gun hard against the lawman's shoulder. 'Nasty place to get a bullet,' he said. 'Now, give me the cell keys.'

Cooper walked straight to the gun rack. He eyed the contents, lifted a short-barrelled scattergun from its box. 'Always wanted to use one o' these bad boys,' he snarled. 'Army never had much use for 'em.'

'The keys,' Lines repeated.

'Go to hell,' Jasper snorted. 'You're not shooting anybody with half the town gathering outside.' He pushed his chair back sharply and raised a hand, trying to knock away the long barrel of the Colt.

But Lines was ready. He took one step back, swung the chamber of the gun hard against the side of Jasper's head.

'I'll bring 'em,' Cooper said. 'They're here with the guns.'

In his cell, Stearne was standing at the door, both hands gripping the bars. When he saw Lines and Cooper, a shade of relief spread across his strained features. 'Where'd the hell you two come from? I thought Byrd had done for both of you.'

'He nearly did. With some help. Now get yourself out of there and fast,' Lines said, as Cooper unlocked the cell door. 'Now we've got to find him.'

Stearne wasn't for arguing. He walked quickly to the front door, stopping momentarily to grab his hat, gun and shoulder holster from the stand.

'Not that way,' Lines warned him. 'The whole goddamn town's baying for your blood.'

Lines waved his Colt towards the back door. 'Through there. It's more fitting for those down on their luck,' he said scornfully.

Cooper snatched up the scattergun, Lines opened the back door and the three men ran out into the back alley. They turned in the direction of the Applejack Room, walking quickly, pausing at every junction that led to the main street.

'How much cash have you got available?' Lines asked Stearne when they were almost opposite the saloon.

'Two or three thousand in the safe. Why?'

'We're leaving town, that's why . . . that's the price. You're all washed up, Stearne. Get used to it. We'll start up somewhere else. Once we grab Byrd.'

★ ★ ★

225

Lines and Cooper ran across the main street. Moments after they disappeared in a side-alley of the saloon, Ruben Byrd and Annie Desmond reined in at the front of the jailhouse.

They tied their mounts to the hitch rail, and Ruben went to the door ahead of Annie.

'It's not going to take long,' he said. 'When we've picked up the two out on the trail, it's more or less over.'

Ruben held the door open and Annie stepped inside. But no sooner had she taken one step forward, than she shrunk back. She pointed to the floor, gave a startled gasp.

'It's George,' she said nervously.

Ruben stepped around her, went quickly to his old friend. He knelt down and turned Jasper on his side, saw the sticky matt of dark blood above his ear.

'Is he dead . . . alive?' Annie started.

'In between. He's still breathing. There's water in the barrel, Annie. Can you bring some?' As Ruben spoke,

Jasper's eyes opened and his hand moved towards his head. Halfway he stopped and winced, uttered a low groan.

'I can see what happened, George. Who the hell did it?' Ruben asked. Without waiting for an answer, he got to his feet and looked to the empty cells.

'Lines an' Cooper,' Jasper growled. 'It was Lines who hit me. Where's Stearne?'

'He's gone.' Ruben hunkered back down, tried to have a closer look at Jasper's head wound. 'You'll live with a headache for a day or two,' he said with a smile. 'Lucky it was your brain box. Someplace else and you'd be in real trouble. Can you get up?'

Annie returned with the water as Jasper got to his feet. He crumpled his features and groaned again.

'I'll be OK. Water won't help much, but thanks, Annie,' he said and took the dipper. 'A few minutes to get my breath an' we'll get going. Take's more than a pistol-whipping to have me say good-night.'

'They'll have gone by now,' Annie said fearfully.

'Not from town they won't,' Ruben corrected. 'They'll be at the saloon . . . where the money is. And they won't be riding anywhere until they've taken care of me.'

'An' they'll kill Stearne . . . the man they know as Fornell,' Jasper put in. 'Rube's worth another grand. That's more'n chicken feed.'

Ruben smiled wryly. As he turned to Annie, he looked more closely at the gun rack on the wall, 'If you had a shotgun, it's not here,' he said to Jasper.

'Cooper took it with him.'

'Yeah, they're in the saloon.' Selecting a Winchester, Ruben checked that it was loaded, and handed it to Annie. 'It's not likely, but if anyone other than me or George comes through that door, pull the trigger. Just like last time,' he said. 'Are you ready, George?'

Jasper nodded, immediately winced.

'Shouldn't do that,' he muttered, walking to the gun rack and pulling out a second Winchester.

Throwing Annie a cautionary glance, Ruben followed him to the door.

The moment the two men were gone, Annie lowered herself into Jasper's chair. *OK, she thought, if that's the way it is. If they're going out to fight, I can play along. I'll shoot if someone even walks past the goddamn window.* She was way past tears now. This was the time for frustration and anger, the icy chill that gripped her stomach.

*   *   *

On the first floor of the Applejack Room, Stearne was standing beside his open safe. He was stuffing bundles of notes into a big bag. Behind him, Lines was watching, anxiously following Stearne's every move. Every few moments, he'd take a look out on to the broad landing where Cooper was standing. He was just outside the door with Jasper's scattergun in a loose 'slope arms' position.

'Byrd's going to be with the Desmond woman,' Stearne said as he layered the cash into the satchel. 'We've got to take care of him, but what about her?'

'I'm sure Coop will think of something,' Lines replied. 'It's that sheriff I'm worried about. Just hurry it up, before someone finds him.'

Stearne stepped away from the safe. He rested the bulging carpet bag on his desk, looked around him as if he knew it was the last time.

Cooper stepped into the doorway. He inclined his head sharply, indicating they should all move out. 'We've been here long enough. Let's get going,' he said.

The three men were almost halfway down the stairs when Jasper and Ruben pushed their way through the saloon doors.

Stearne was the first to see them and

turning back, he almost collided with Lines.

'Back,' he shouted. 'It's them. Byrd and Jasper.'

Lines shoved the saloon owner aside, swung his gun around.

'There's no way out,' Jasper shouted. 'Drop your guns.'

The handful of customers that were at the bar dropped their drinks. They didn't run, just moved awkwardly for the doors. Harry the barman backed off along the bar. Cursing, he slipped a hand below the counter for his scattergun.

Lines's and Jasper's guns fired simultaneously. But Jasper was more ready, his aim more controlled, and his bullet hit Lines square in the chest.

Lines staggered, putting a hand out for support. The Colt in his other hand continued to fire, but his fingers weren't in control and he'd lost his way.

Behind him, Cooper raised the shotgun. Holding the gun tight against his hip, and cursing obscenities, he fired down to the floor below him, towards Ruben and Jasper.

Ruben raised his .44 Navy Colt, held it firmly in a two-handed grip, aimed carefully and pulled the trigger.

A dark hole blossomed in Cooper's shirt front. He went back, up a single step, then forward, down again, watching mystified as the shotgun dropped from his fingers. He grunted, snatched at the makeshift sling across his chest, wanting free of it for some futile reason. Then his legs buckled and he fell headlong, almost making it to the saloon floor.

Resting against the handrail of the wide staircase, Lines was still on his feet. With a mean grin at Ruben, he aimed the Colt he'd taken from Jasper's desk.

Ruben shook his head. 'Your last battle,' he mouthed and fired one more time.

As the smoke cleared, and Jasper went to check on the two bodies, Ruben made his way quickly from the saloon. He pushed decisively through the ornate doors to the boardwalk and stopped, looked to his left and right, through the keyed-up mill of saloon customers. Then he rushed back into the saloon, crossed straight to one of the heavy drapes and through to the open back door.

He realized that Stearne wasn't up in his office, and certainly wouldn't stay there. The man would leave the building by way of his covert staircase at the rear of the building.

He was right. Stearne was trying to fix his carpet bag to one of a few customer horses that were standing in the rear yard of the building.

Ruben virtually sprang the distance between them. 'No one's likely to take any notice of this,' he said, shoving the barrel of his Colt hard into the middle of Stearne's back. 'You will, and it'll be the last thing you ever hear.'

'There's a couple of thousand dollars here. It's all yours if you walk away. No one's going to know. Say I was gone before you could do anything,' Stearne proposed.

In reply, Ruben transferred the Colt to his left hand. He took half a step back, drove his fist hard into Stearne's kidneys. 'Fall down, and you'll never get up. I promise,' he threatened savagely.

Stearne gasped for air. He slumped forward, his face buried in the bag of money.

'It's a shame all the good men who'd want to see you gargling on a rope, are dead,' Ruben said. 'That includes a couple of bad ones. At least we all know the truth, you son-of-a-bitch.'

'You out here stamping on bugs?' George Jasper said tiredly as he stepped down from the saloon into the yard.

'Just the one.'

'You know where we're going, tinhorn. Give me any trouble and I'll do worse than Byrd ever would,' Jasper warned Stearne.

As the sheriff and his prisoner disappeared along the alley, Ruben's gun hand dropped. He took off his hat, with the crook of his arm smoothed his long, fair hair across the top of his head. He took a deep breath, then followed on to the main street.

He'd turned towards the jailhouse when Annie Desmond came running towards him.

'Where the hell were you?' he asked with a straight face. 'We were in real trouble back there.'

'I was crying too much to be of any help,' she replied. Tears of relief were glistening in her eyes.

Ruben put his arm around her shoulders, and oblivious to the people watching, they walked off down the street.

After a few paces, Ruben realized he was still gripping his Colt. 'One of you's got to go,' he said.

'Assuming it's not going to be me, what would you do if you didn't wear a gun?' Annie asked.

'Well, I had wondered about invest-ing in some kind of breakfast cart. A chuck wagon for town folk, but offering steak, eggs and coffee.'

'How will that work, then?'

'I'll have the smithy find me an old mud wagon. With a few modifications, I'll have it parked up under the cottonwood. If what most folk are saying's true, Annie, there's going to be small fortunes made here.'

We do hope that you have enjoyed reading this large print book.

Did you know that all of our titles are available for purchase?

We publish a wide range of high quality large print books including:
Romances, Mysteries, Classics
General Fiction
Non Fiction and Westerns

Special interest titles available in large print are:
The Little Oxford Dictionary
Music Book, Song Book
Hymn Book, Service Book

Also available from us courtesy of Oxford University Press:
Young Readers' Dictionary
(large print edition)
Young Readers' Thesaurus
(large print edition)

For further information or a free brochure, please contact us at:
Ulverscroft Large Print Books Ltd.,
The Green, Bradgate Road, Anstey,
Leicester, LE7 7FU, England.
Tel: (00 44) 0116 236 4325
Fax: (00 44) 0116 234 0205

Neither Rafe Charnley nor his son Jeff could have foreseen how quickly their family tensions would escalate when Jeff falls in love with the daughter of the sheepherders with whom the family have a long-standing feud. Rafe cannot see his son's actions as anything but a deeply personal betrayal. Jeff is desperate to prove his feelings to his father — but when his beau's brother is accused of violating a land boundary, Rafe threatens to have him strung up. Can the hostilities between them be rectified without blood being spilled?

McGRAW RETURNS

J. W. Throgmorton

Twenty years in prison tamed Jack McGraw, or so he thought. He returns to Crockett, Texas, where he meets his daughter, Rebecca, for the first time, and discovers that he must save her and their farm from Ben Page. Unknown to Rebecca, Page has found crude oil on an unused part of the farm. A sample sent to Pittsburg confirmed its value, and Page alone knows it's worth millions. He sends his henchmen to kidnap Rebecca, and soon McGraw finds himself on a three-state rescue mission . . .

THE VINDICATORS

Brent Larssen

In the summer of 1879, young Ben Drake travels to the town of Mason in New Mexico. The eighteen-year-old aims to find out the truth about his father's death at the hands of a lynch mob, but soon finds his own life endangered as he is drawn into the Mason County War. A band of young men are challenging the iron rule of businessman Angus McBride, who has the authorities at his beck and call. Calling themselves the Vindicators, they find themselves fighting against a troop of US Cavalry . . .

PACK TRAIN

Greg Mitchell

Scott Bailey's first day with a US Government pack train nearly becomes his last day on earth. Narrowly escaping an ambush, he soon experiences other attempts on his life. Soon he finds himself embroiled in a dangerous situation involving law officers, military men and renegades, and suspects that he is being used as bait to trap the leader of a criminal operation. Scott teams up with Maley, a government investigator, and together they work to destroy the operation — but the unknown leader remains at large . . .

A DUELLIST IN KANSAS

Tom R. Wade

British Army officer John Carshalton is serving in Canada when he gets into a battle with a Frenchman over the affections of a woman. The dispute ends with Carshalton killing his rival in an illegal duel, and he must flee south of the border to escape court martial. He finds himself in a small Kansas town near Abilene, where he makes a victorious stand with an ageing deputy sheriff against a group of outlaws. But the murdered Frenchman's brother is after him, intent on forcing him into one more duel . . .